# REDUCTION OF THE IMPOTENT.

## a fairy-tale by

# TIGER MOODY

a **United Crud** book
NEW YORK, NEW YORK

Copyright 2013, 2015, 2018 Tiger Moody
This edition © 2018 United Crud
All rights reserved.
ISBN: 0-9965110-7-5
ISBN-13: 978-0-9965110-7-0
*For Mildred & Thurston !*

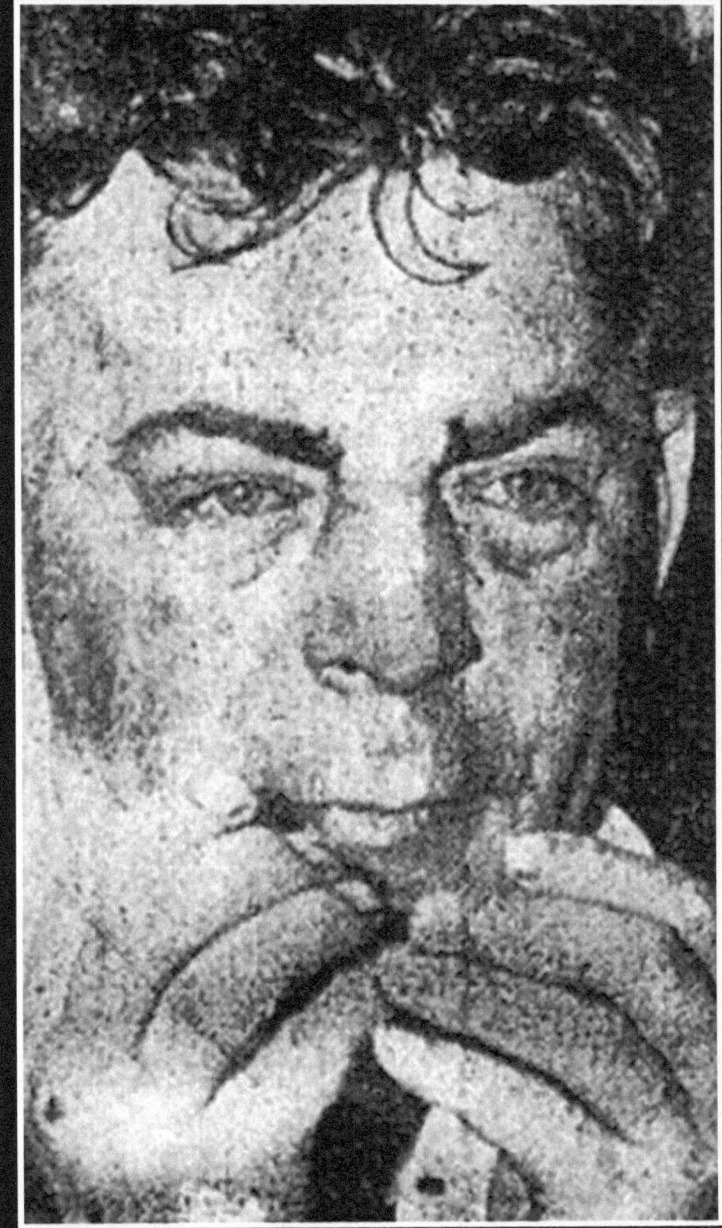

"And I verily do suppose that in the braines and hertes of children, which be membres spirituall, whiles they be tender, and the little slippes of reason begynne in them to bud, ther may happe by evil custome some pestiferous dewe of vice to perse the sayde membres, and infecte and corrupt the soft and tender buddes."
— Sir Thomas Eliot (1531)

**AUTUMN, '53, MANHATTAN** — a whit shy of 33rd.

Spying a blonde with child amidst dawn's crush, Jack Coal felt abdominal twinges. Though she was young, winsome, and bosomy, he was too absorbed by the tiny pained mien for such virtues to anchor and flourish. Drawn tight — its features were furrowed, damp, vermillion. How very salty might those tears taste were he to kneel & kiss them away?

Pangs continued to gnaw.

A tongueflick freed a molar's ham paste.

Ignoring a reciprocal smirk...surveying a rectangular Elgin...Jack Coal hurried ahead.

**THE LAFARGUE CLINIC** — a blandly finished cluster clogging the basement of Saint Philip's Episcopal — was captained by an aging headshrinker named Fredric Thaddeus Wertham.

While Dr. Wertham was hoary & slight, the old man was by no means frail; on the contrary, he was fueled by a vigor bordering continuous rage. This innerfire had blossomed in Flanders — where he'd slaughtered nine AEF soldiers; medals were secured within the bottom left-drawer of an immaculate walnut desk.

Across this desk sat a small Puerto Rican who looked six but was actually nine. Somehow silent despite tear-restraint, Luis was suspected of shoving a child off the ledge of a tenement-roof.

A red towel had encircled the body's limp neck.

Lenses boosting irides to Martian-proportions filled the small boy with terror. That the old man rasped with a Prussian inflection only heightened this tension. Luis's father had been castrated by Nazis — Huns stormed dreams almostnightly. Even the sight of warm sauerkraut was sufficent to trigger damp fits.

Standing abruptly, approaching a window, Dr. Wertham wrenched drapery aside. Upon Harlem concrete, a crowned black man guided leashed leopards.

Sighing, the old man yanked the drapes shut.

"Please, Luis...what you must understand is that I'm not here to hurt you...nor to make you feel badly...I simply want to know WHY this happened! That's what we all want to know! We want to get to the bottom of this! We want to help you! Make things all better! Not just for you...but for many people! For everybody!"

Remaining mum, spying dull carpet, Luis focused

upon streetbleats adrift, promising himself that one day he too would steer Checkers. Honk horns all'a damn time! While Luis had not yet explored a taxicab's innards...riding only on buses & subways...someday — someday things would be different!

The small boy glanced drapewards, discovering only thin air. Claws falling vised rear-shoulders.

"Young man, I shall now share some of my research!"

From the desktop, Dr. Wertham lifted a narrow notebook similar to those of peaceofficers. Masking lips with a gnarled fist, his throat emitted a queer phlegmless hack. Luis had once heard an ostrich make such noises whilst visiting the Central Park Zoo — the same day he'd seen a chimpanzee ejaculate.

1) A boy of six wrapped his throat with an old sheet then jumped from the rafter of a Wisconsin barn. His brother later testified that such behavior had been absorbed from a crime comic book called 'Jughead'.

2) A twelve year-old boy was found hanged by a clothesline tossed over a shower- rod. His mother told the jury that she thought he had been re-enacting a scene from the Tarzan comic books he'd incessantly read. The jury returned a verdict of accidental-death then scorned both comics and Tarzan.

3) A boy was found dead in the bathroom wearing a Superman costume. He had stran-gled himself while trying to walk on the walls of the room like his hero.

4) A boy of ten accidentally hanged himself while playing 'hanging'. He will never play

this game again.

5) A twelve year-old boy was found hanging naked from a door hook suspended by his bathrobe-cord. On the floor under his open hand lay a comic book with this cover: a girl on a horse with a noose around her neck, the rope tied to a tree. A laughing man was leading the horse away, tightening the noose as he did so. The grief-stricken father said, 'The boy was happy when I saw him last. I'll be damned if I ever allow another comic book in this house! They are the Devil's tennis-racquet and the children are his unwitting balls!'

6) A boy of eleven was found hanged naked from a rope in the bathroom. He had a habit of acting out comic book stories. He allegedly once lit his babysitter on fire while she slept. He is said to have been naked then too.

7) A boy of thirteen named Roy was found hanged in the garage. On the floor was a comic book showing a hanging and a stack of his sister's underpants. On the wall, written in chalk, was a crude self-portrait above the phrase 'KILL ROY HERE!'

8) A ten year-old was found unconscious hanging from a 2nd-story balcony. This idea came from an adored comic book story. Once revived, he expressed genuine dismay that Captain Marvel had not rescued him as he was the regional fan-club president.

9) A boy died after swinging in a noose from a tree. He had tried to show another boy 'how

people hang themselves to get high.' The City
Council denounced the 'mind-warping'
influence of comic books.

10) A gifted Oriental, aged just eight, leapt
from a San Francisco fire-escape 'like Superman' only to break both wrists. His promising
career as a violinist was likewise shattered.

**SHELVING THE NOTEBOOK**, swiping lenses with
linen, Dr. Wertham addressed the small boy.

"So then...does ANY of this sound familiar to you?"

Though tears now flowed freely, Luis's quietude endured. A swath was thrust forwards.

Its monogram burned the boy's eyes.

F   T   W

"Please understand...I am here only to help! Together, we will get you THROUGH this!"

Clear snotstreams seeping from nostrils piled atop
pink gabardine. The old man smiled kindly.

"Keep that hanky, Luis! Consider it a souvenir!"

**HIS BOOK DECREED DEFUNCT** that morning,
Jack Coal was gripped by nearstroke. Blood seized
in veins. Testes knotted to a monkey's fist. A Stetson slipped free of limp hands. Slumping down to a
cracked wooden stool, he slowly began to die.

Will Meiser, a balding pipesmoker, attempted to
smear fatherly comfort despite being six years junior.

"Jackie m'boy, look at it THIS way — you've had a
terrific run! Thirteen years is nothin' to sneeze at! But
the times...the times they are achangin'!"

Staring off to a sill's graveyard, Jack Coal pondered
assgluing inked Kleenex to a horsefly many years pri-
or. The studio had roared while the insect had buzzed

imploring all to DRINK PEPSI-COLA! — even
Meiser, a man of small humor, releasing a few wheezy
sniggers. A tinge of sadness had overtaken the room
when the furious pitchman had finally escaped onto
East Forty First — merging with the chaos beneath.

Jack Coal wondered where the fly had expired. Over
the Hudson, he hoped. The thought possessed some
inexplicably dignified shred.

"Listen, Jackie...don't see this as the end...look at it as
a new opportunity! A new beginning! A reawakening
of sorts! It's not like I'm canning you....there's plenty
of other work! Elastic Man was truly great, but...
it's just...these kids...they don't want colored pajamas
anymore! Stuff's SEEN its day! What sells now is lust,
blood, guts, horror! Scientific Fiction! Saucers!
Vampires! Ghouls! That sorta blote..."

Jack Coal studied livery palmversos already doppel-
gänging his grandfather's. A deep breath was stowed
'til blood again crept, but the monkey held fast — his
testicles still throbbed. He wondered what blote
meant. Why did Jews so often address him in Yid-
dish? Did he look Jewish — or was it simply because
they're so pushy? "But Will...I know all that! I do pay
attention and I've done every darned thing you've
asked! Thrown in every bloodsucker, dopepeddler &
whiteslaver you've requested! I've spiced things up
plenty and I'm willing to up the ante even more! But
Elastic Man...he's the hero of millions! The children
still love him! If any pajamaboy can survive this — it's
him! He's elastic for Pete's sake! He can literally change
WITH the times! Chazzers in dreck — remember?
Think of the children, Will! The children'll cry!"

Desperate to palliate, Will Meiser rubbed slumped shoulders like a Turkish bath's insensate Swede.

"Jackie...hate to be blunt...but let's talk brasstacks here...your book hasn't cracked two hundred kay since the war ended! Even those shtuppies are outselling Elastic Man now! More GIRLS are buying St. John's romance-crap than boys are Green Weevil & Captain Blammo combined! And let's face it, Jack...the boys drive the business! You know that!"

Toes curled within lifeless Florsheims.

"Yeah, I know..."

"Heck, man...makes ya feel any better, I'm even sending The Apparition to the moon! IMAGINE THAT! Makes me sick...really it does...but I just dunno what else to do! Tried it all!"

Jack Coal gaped north astonished.

Penned by the bald man himself, a cartoonist of unique elan, THE APPARITION was the industry's lone ray of hope. Unlike other titles, it wasn't disseminated via spinning-rack but inserted directly in papers themselves — a sui generis arrangement!

Comic books were for children...

The funnypages were for adults...

This was a comic book WITHIN the funnIes!

A comic book for adults — the only beast of its kind!

And now this cockamamie fool's fourcolor seppuku was supposed to make Jack Coal feel better?!!

**POST ARMY-INDUCTION,** Jack Coal became his employer's ghost — birthing double workdays and pursuant fatigue. Three weeks into this new routine, he'd fallen asleep atop shepherd's pie; crushing a nose & spec-lenses.

Despite Dot's urges of moderation, Jack Coal sidestepped...he'd solemnly vowed to nurse an orphan — was he not a man of his word?

His complexion soon dulled to translucence. His sloop drastically worsened. He'd even drawn barefoot near a bucket of ice — hypothermically shocking when eyelids faltered.

But the situation had not been devoid of rewards. Manning The Apparition had been the proudest moment of a shoddy career. He'd taken great pains to maintain a look and, by gum, he'd succeeded — only the astutest of readers discerning a slight tonal-variance. It was as if is boss had never donned drab.

As if Meiser no longer mattered.

The bald man's death was daydreamed a thousand times over. Sometimes in France. Sometimes in Burma. Once, even in Butte. The results, however, were always the same:

A mine. A blast. A meerschaum airborne.

**UPON AN UNSCATHED '46 RETURN**, Meiser resumed The Apparition's helm, fusing reinvigorated strokes with satanic layouts to skipper unchartered heights. The stories were taut, grim, muscular, dire. If anyone had ever mistaken the book for kidfare, this would never happen again. Even begrudging highbrows had to admit that this was indeed ART!

Regarding these pages with abject awe, Jack Coal realized his error — Will Meiser DID matter. Inquiring after this wellspring's source, the bald man had reached within a vicuna topcoat to draw a linty handful of pills.

**IN 1949 THE MEISER STUDIO** signed a lucrative contract with the US Army. As illiteracy had gone viral within the infantry's rapid expansion, General MacArthur had decreed instructional comics be issued alongside field-manuals. Tackling the new job personally, Meiser assigned Apparitional duties to an assembly of writers, pencilers & inkers — a force uninclusive of Jack Coal.

Despite this painful slight, the ex-ghost endured mum; carping not being his style.

The following summer, at a July Fourth mixer, the lumbering teetotalist had absorbed three punches before discovering their tainted nature. By then, however, it was far too late — his boss had already been cornered.

"Was it...because my work was subpar?"

Welling eyes trailed a hasty embrace. There was a Mothicide-scent to the bald man's suit; just a faint trace — but Jack Coal was certain Dot would detect it. The only things she disliked more than mothballs were Communists & the Democratic Party.

Rearing orbs were gently dabbed with a corner of mandarin silk. "Jack, is that really what you thought? Really? Good GOD, man! How many times must I tell you this? Second to me — you're the shop's MVP! Couldn't afford to waste your talents on some dying gig... only a shmeggege would do that!"

Jack Coal stood wavering — speechless —

flabbergasted. How could this silly bald man find him so damned important? He simply wasn't an important person! And why would he refer to The Apparition as a dying feature? As far as he could tell, the book was as good as it'd ever been! Better!

"Jackie, listen...ELASTIC MAN is a very special thing — you're doing something unique here! Something unprecedented! Something...perhaps even historic..."

Jowls waggled left then right.

"C'mon, Will — don't try'n josh me! What YOU do is great! I know it...you know it...everybody knows it! It is what it is! But MY work? Pretty much everyone else's? It's...it's GARBAGE! Elastic Man's garbage! Superman's garbage! The Batman...he's garbage too! WE are garbage! We draw stickmen on ragpaper for snotnosed brats and incestuous, drooling morons! Sorry, Will...sorry to babble...very embarrassed...but...I...I...I just...really enjoyed working on The Apparition. Just made me feel a little bit less...like...garbage."

Mottled scalpflesh tilted & shook.

"Jack...I'm saddened to hear that's how you feel. Hope that's just the punch talking."

From an interior-pocket, the bald man retrieved a tarry pipe then swirled it within oiled leather. Stoking the bowl, he drew — exhaling sugary clouds.

"No siree, certainly hope not! Jackie...when you hand me a pile of fresh pages, they sure

don't look like they were drawn by someone
who feels that way! No sir! No sir indeed!
They strike me as the toil of someone who
packs a HELLUVA lotta energy, imagination &
love into their craft! Like they were drawn by
someone who cares! 'Garbage' would be just
about the furthest thing from what
you've lain across my desk!"

　Shame-deluged, Jack Coal quaked.

　Shouldn't have said nothing...

　"Jackie, don'tcha listen to anyone else!
Regardless of whether they're too stupid to
realize it, what you do is very, very important! You're just as important to society as any
fireman, policeman, doctor, or lawyer! Maybe
even more so! Think on it...you've made a
million kids happy every month! How many
others can say that? Made 'em as happy as
chazzers in dreck! And, guess what? It's ART,
goddamnit! It's ART, Jack, despite what a million squares will try and feed ya! You're a real
artist...and...someday — everyone will agree!"

　Head hung, the inebriate sighed. "But...but
what about the drooling morons?"

**RISING SWIFT, VISING ARMTWEED**, Jack Coal
stammered insensibly before a shocked glare triggered
release. The bald man rubbed a tenderized bicep.

　"Will...sir...please! Let ME handle The Apparition
in Space! If Elastic Man is getting nixed anyway,
perhaps there's some kinda tie-in there? A noble end!
Killed by a wayward meteorite? Or...or maybe he leaps
into the path of some Martian raybeam aimed at The

Apparition? Gets vaporized in the process? Some kinda noble end! Y'know...something dignified!"

Clucks accented weary headshakes.

"Oy...getting VAPORIZED is dignified?"

"Or something! Will...please! Lemme end it upbeat!"

The bald dome continued to wag as a sleeve was palmed smooth. "Won't wash, Jackie...hired a new boy to handle it...just focus on making that last Elastic Man a gentle goodbye for all the old fans. You can cut the tits and blood outta this one...something sweet... maybe a little bit sad. Gimme some vintage Jack Coal! Do your own thing! Just do what makes ya YOU!"

Despite a mien perfectly blank — inside Jack Coal things were different. He was not feeling sweet & maybe a little bit sad. He was feeling murderous.

As he strolled off puffing, Meiser winked.

Gripping a t-square, Jack Coal pondered cracked sternums. Bet his heart tastes of greenbacks.

"Who...Will? Who? Who IS this new guy?"

Still shaking circulation into his arm, the bald man grinned as he approached officeclutter. "Young boychik, nicelookin' fella! Ex-paratrooper! Good!"

Gnawing a lip, Jack Coal nodded.

"Oh...he's good then, huh?"

"Well, yes...yes he is! Very, very good! But that's not what I meant! That's his NAME — Wallace Good!"

A slam left Jack Coal staring at a closed door.

A glass pane one might spy through.

**HORN & HARDART'S WAS LARGE** and bright-lit — lined with walls of tokenstarved cubes, each housing greasetopped Fiesta. Long tables flanked by riveted benches aped a prison's messhall. The room brimmed codgers and miscreants; half screaming for reasons unknown forced the residuum to likewise compete. While most Meiserians lunched in bars with free beef, Bert Meskin tended to shadow Jack Coal as faithfully as a huntsman's beagle.

Freshly released from six weeks in Bellevue, the frail man struggled to hold food aloft.

Jesus, ninth time in less than ten years.

Jack Coal ideated Mrs. Meskin's grief.

And with all those poor kids to feed too...

Now he'd returned with a stutter. He'd never stuttered before. Surveying his friend's slight frame, he wondered if ghosts donned bowties in Hell.

"Buddy...whatizzit? Tuna turned? Barely touched it!"

Lifting the sandwich, extracting a nibble, Bert Meskin feebly chewed. "N-n-n-n-no, s-s'good. I l-l-l-like it...r-r-r-really!"

Shrugging, Jack Coal resumed burgerfocus until his mass was no more. Glancing across the table again, he nodded towards untended remains. "Mind if I...?"

"N-n-n-n-n-no, Jack! T-t-t-t-take it! J-j-just n-not h-h-hungry, I g-g-guess!"

Within four chomps, the sandwich was gone — but still Jack Coal hungered. He felt as though he might consume a wedding-banquet — parson & flowergirl inclusive. He'd felt that way for some years now, a mare's nest echoed by chins.

He'd been so skinny in his youth.

Positively reedthin...

**From whence this vacuity stemmed eluded. The mystery irked. He didn't like it. And certainly, neither did Dot. She'd recently asked if he'd noted grey pubes.**

"Haha...really? Nope! Hmmn...age, with his stealing steps, hath clawed me in his clutch!"

A returnglare had beamed pure disgust.

"If your goddamned stomach wasn't so bloated, you mighta seen. I have a few too — not that you woulda noticed those either..."

He'd smiled, armcoiling a waist still waspish.

"Hon, sorry if I haven't been as attentive as I ought to've been. Just that...just that I've been workin' so darn hard lately! I just...just...WANT THINGS for you! Wantcha to have everything you deserve...and I'm gonna make sure you get it all too! You're gonna have that darn house in Connecticut even if it kills me first!"

Emerald orbs disdainfully rolled.

"You mean 'us'..."

"Yes, that's EXACTLY what I mean! Us! Gazebo in the back! Weekends at the club! The works! I want all of that for you! For...US!"

A tapered pointer sank in his belly all the way to the second small knuckle.

"Speaking of clubs...why not dust off your set and take them up to Van Cortlandt this Sunday? Been ages, dear...you could really use some sun! Don't like you being indoors so much! Not healthy!"

He'd nodded and smiled. She'd given him a sack of Wright & Ditsons for his thirty-fifth —

proudly boasting of their Lindbergh-endorse-
ment. Despite leaving the house tammed on
several occasions, he'd never actually set foot
on a green. He hated golf. So much walking.

**AS CHOWDER DRAINED** like lemonade, the frail
man grinned at his chum. "J-J-J-J-J-Jack. I-I-I-I-I'm
s-s-sorry...b-b-b-but...I have a qu-qu-qu-question..."
   Lowering the mug, toweling his maw —
Jack Coal recoiled from red smears.
   "Ask me no questions and I'll tell you no lies!"
   "S-s-s-sorry, J-J-Jack..."
   "Bert, cryin' out loud — kidding! Whatizzit? Prob-
lems at home? Anything I can help with — here for
ya! ALWAYS...Bert...hope y'know that!"
   "I-I-I-I-I d-d-do, Jack! I d-d-d-d-do know th-that!
A-a-a-a-a-and I a-a-appre-preciate it! A l-l-l-l-l-l-lot!"
   A brow's narrow boosted steelrims. "Anything
CREEPY happen in there? Something...unethical?"
   "N-n-no, Jack! N-n-n-not exactly! B-b-b-b-b-but
y-y-yes, k-k-kinda! J-J-J-J-Jack...you ev-ever h-h-
heard of D-D-D-D-Doctor W-W-Werth-th-th-tham?"
   "WERTHAM? Can't say I have! Odd name, think I
would remember it! This fellow do something offkey?"
   "N-n-n-no, not ex-exac-t-t-ly! H-h-h-h-he's a psy-
psy-psychi-chi-chiatrist from G-G-G-G-Germany,
I-I-I-I think! He v-v-v-visit-t-t-ted us in the h-h-h-
hosp-p-pital! H-h-h-h-he was m-m-m-mainly w-w-
work-k-k-ing in the j-j-j-j-juven-n-n-nile w-w-w-
ward — b-b-but w-when he f-f-f-found out I was in
the c-c-c-c-comic b-b-b-b-books, he w-w-w-wanted
to sp-speak with m-m-me t-t-t-t-too!"
   "Well? Yeah? And what'd he wanna know?"

"J-J-J-Jack...it was b-b-bad! V-v-very b-b-b-bad!
H-h-h-h-he w-w-wanted to kn-kn-know what I-I-I
th-thought — m-m-m-my op-p-p-p-pin-pin-pinions!
H-h-h-h-he w-wanted to kn-kn-kn-know if I-I-I th-
th-th-thought I was h-h-h-h-hurting k-k-k-k-kids!"
Testes knotted and throbbed.

"Hurting kids? What's that mean? Why would he
think you're hurting KIDS? How? Bert, I'm confused!"

"He...h-h-h-h-h-he...he runs a cl-cl-clin-n-n-ic up in
H-H-H-H-Harlem and he's b-b-been d-d-d-doing a
st-st-study on th-th-th-the influ-flu-flu-ence of c-c-c-
c-comics on j-j-j-j-juvenn-n-nile d-d-d-d-delin-quen-
quen-cy! I-I-I'm s-s-s-s-sorry, J-J-J-J-Jack!"

Pain increasing, Jack Coal shifted in a vain attempt
to ease pressure. "Heck — Bert, calm down! Don't
be sorry, you've done nothin' wrong! Knew something like this would happen eventually...it was only
a matter of time! This is a crummy, garbage industry
we're stuck in! Strictly for birds! Garbage! Shoulda
never lost sight of syndication! Once I had a few bucks
socked, shoulda begged-off Meiser's and given it a
genuine stab! Been another Bushmiller! BUSHMILL-
ER has class! Bushmiller drives a Packard!"

"M-m-m-m-m-me t-t-t-t-too! I-I-I-I sh-sh-sh-
should h-have t-t-t-t-too, J-J-Jack!"

Ignoring his friend, Jack Coal turned to face an
elderly hag snoring beside macaroni. Her skin, oily &
green, stirred recalls of youthnetted catfish.

"Well, what's this Wertham-character planning to
DO with this research...or did he not even say?"

"A-a-a-a-a b-b-b-book! An art-t-t-ticle or a b-b-b-b-
b-book, I th-th-think!"

"Cripes...great!"

"J-J-J-Jack. I'm...I-I-I-I'm s-s-s-s-sorry to say this, b-b-b-b-but he had some c-c-c-c-comics with him! S-s-s-s-some he ask-sk-sked me a-a-about! A-a-a-a-a f-f-f-few of th-them — a f-f-f-few of th-th-them — w-w-w-w-w-were y-y-y-y-yours!"

"Judas Priest, Bert! This ain't good...not good at all! Any Elastic Mans?"

"Y-y-y-y-yes, o-o-one or t-t-t-two — but th-th-there was a c-c-c-c-c-crime b-b-b-b-book too! A-a-a-about a g-g-girl and a d-d-dope r-r-ring f-f-from a f-few y-years b-b-b-back! I-i-i-i-i-it w-w-w-wasn't s-s-signed...b-b-b-but I knew it was y-y-yours b-b-be-cause I in-in-in-inked the b-b-b-back-gr-gr-grounds!"

Hands spread cloaked a pained sigh.

"God...MURDEROUS MORPHINE & I, correct?"

"Y-y-y-y-yeah...y-yes..."

"Christ! Fucking Meiser! Really pushed me on that one too! Even then, I knew it was too much! The kids want more crime! The kids want more sex! Dope! Rape! Kill! Shoulda told him to get stuffed a long time back! Know what he did today, Bert? Know what that mothbally HEEB did today?"

"W-w-w-w-what d-d-d-did he d-d-d-do, J-J-J-Jack?"

"HE FUCKING CANCELLED ELASTIC MAN!"

"Oh g-g-g-gosh! Th-th-th-th-that's b-b-b-b-baaaad news, Jack! Awful s-s-s-sorry!"

Annexing the Greek's cold macaroni, Jack Coal brayed through wan pap. "Tell me about it! What am I gonna say to DOT? That book pays our rent!"

Perking, Bert Meskin raised a finger. "G-g-g-g..."

"Buddy, try not to think so hard! Just let it roll out!"

. "G-G-G-G-GOLDFISH!"

"Goldfish?"

"Y-Y-Y-Y-Y-Y-Y-YES! G-G-G-G-G-GOLDFISH!"

A next-tabled child sucking beans through a straw suddenly transfixed Jack Coal. "Honestly, Bert — that's the dumbest thing I ever heard!"

**"LIKE ALL DEM CRIME COMICS** — all kinda comic books really! Science ones! ANDY PANDA! BUSTA CRABBE! All a'em! Buy quite a few! Get 'em from friends! Some give 'em t'me...some loan 'em! CLUE's a real goody! S'all about when dis fella — he and t'ree otha men — dey robbed some jewelry n'took rings and den run away n'dis cop's car came and den dey plugged 'em! Sometimes d'cops ice d'gangstas — sometimes d'hoods off d'cops!"

The old man stared from behind his desk.

His patient — six feet/mustachioed/muscled — claimed to be only twelve. "Ma don' like me readin' comics no mores — but I sees 'em anyhows! SUPAH-MAN! PENALTY! JUMBO! Love me dem JUM-BO-books! Lotsa swell broads in dere! Lotsa scraps! Men rumblin' wimmen! Sometimes dey kills d'broads! Strangle 'em! Shoot 'em! Sometimes dey poison 'em! In dat magazine JUMBO — dey stab 'em lots too! D'broads don't do much stabbin' — mostly jus' gets stabbed deyselves! But sometimes d'broads stab d'men n'sometimes even plugs 'em good too! Even read one book wheres dey ties people t'trees den cut branches so d'sap runs all ovah n'den d'bugs goes t'woik! Some-times dey torture broads too! T'rows 'em inta rivahs t'make 'em swim where all dem big gaytahs play! Don't have much rags on when dey do dat! Sights me quite a bit, dat stuff!"

Betwixt steepled digits, Dr. Wertham yawned.

"Floyd...this excites you HOW precisely?"

"Scuse me?"

"In what way do these comics STIMULATE you? Do they stir your emotions or imagination? Do they provoke penile-erections?"

"Eh, I...um...dunno...dey jus'...make me...like, feel HAPPY I guess, y'know? Sometimes I got a lot on my mind and dey jus'...like...kinda help me fuhget..."

"So — they provide ESCAPISM?"

Youthful palms shot north. "Uh-uh! No sir! No how! When dey sent me up t'Warwick — I ain't NEVAH tried no 'scapes! Did my bit fair'n'square!"

Denosing glasses, sighing, the old man compressed temples fraught. "You mean: to escape..."

"Yeah...dat's what I said! NEVAH! But in some books — dey shows ya how!"

"Shows you how to what?"

"T'SCAPE!"

Opening his policeman's log, Dr. Wertham scribbled. "And what else do these JUMBO-books teach?"

"Lotsa t'ings! All sortsa shit! Boostin'! Killin'! But I read othas also! My sis buys romance books! I read 'em too! DIARY OF REAL LIFE! SHEENA! Boy, dem can get real sightin' sometimes! Kick men down, chop 'em all up! Make a guy yuk n'yuk! I also like PENALTY! CRIMINALS NEVAH WIN too! But I don' like how d'crooks allus gets caught! Wanna see 'em get away — like in real life! Least dey some-times show some kinky stuff! Like in dis one book, dis broad walks inta dis store and takes dis dress

·n'walks right out n'dis bigass dagga jus'...like...friggin'
KIBOSHES her! Love t'see broads catchin' broads!
Lady-cops! Yes! Want 'em t'frisk me too! N'Sheena...
woah...headlights...oh brotha! WOWIEWOWWOW!
VAVAVOOM! Knows what I mean? When I gets ready
t'hit d'hay, I likes t'read 'bout four or five a dem! Helps
'cause I's hungry lotta nights n'takes d'ol' mind off
d'gut! We don' alla time got chow t'eat 'cause ma
ain't often got dough!"

A frosty brow narrowed & knotted.

"Your mother doesn't have enough money to feed
you and your sister? Does she not know about govern-
ment-relief? And where, may I ask, is your father?"

"Ah...he bought it back in the war!"

"Your father bought WHAT in the war?"

"Nip grenade! On sale 'cause d'pin was missin'!"

Once again, a pen scribbled.

**ALTHOUGH DOT SMIRKED** upon the small
globe's reveal, within eyes lurked deep suspicion. Two
goldfish lay passively adrift — one a dull saffron,
the other ivory with carbon smears.

"Couldn't you've just bought two YELLOW ones?"

"But, then...then we wouldn't be able to tell 'em apart.
The spotted one's you! Spots...Dot! Get it?"

"Yeah...I get it, Jack. You're the yellow one, of course."

Gently accepting the vessel, Dot set it upon the diningroom table then pecked Jack Coal's left cheek.

"Thanks, dear — they're lovely."

As his wife returned to the kitchen to chop,
Jack Coal frowned at the fish.

**HE WAITED 'TIL LATER** to broach the kibosh
— supper being pot-roast with fingerlings, he didn't
want to spoil the mood. Instead they bandied rustic
pie-safes and Colonial saltbox-houses — both current
obsessions of Dot. Afterwards they perched on the
sofa for Godfrey while Dot knitted & he browsed the
evening-edition. When she queried his day during a
commercial-break, he knew better than to beat
about bushes. "And...that...that's it?"

Myopic vision paperglued, Jack Coal wearily
shrugged. "But hon...what could I do? Meiser's the
boss y'know. Say...lookee here! Electroluxes halfoff!"

A glare lingered and raked.

"The...boss? This little man...this KIKE...nixes thirteen years of blood, sweat & tears and all you can say
is well he's the boss? That's really all you have to
say about this? No, Jack! No! We've worked far too
hard — you simply can't allow this to stand! No! You
will not because I will not let you! No! En-oh! No!"

"But hon..."

"No, Jack — NO! You're to inform him tomorrow
that under no circumstances will you accept this!
That you're prepared to take Elastic Man to a different house if need be! He simply cannot do this to us!
You're forty one years-old, Jack! I am forty one years-
old! There's no starting over! No second chances!
You can't let this Jew ruin us!"

"But hon, it's not so simple. Meiser owns the character...I explained all this years back. All of the material
produced by the shop is his outright possession."

"So? So what? So we'll buy the goddamn rights from
Meiser and take it to another shop after! Though it

strikes me as silly we'd even have to! After all, YOU created Elastic Man, Jack — it's yours by moral-rights! He might even just give it to you! Didja ever thinka that? Wouldn't that be the right thing to do? You call him your friend, do you not?"

"But hon, please, there's more to it then — "

As Dot covered her face, inhaling labored and deep, Jack Coal watched Julius LaRosa rhapsodize over blues lowdown & dirty. "Well...what about that KURTZSTEIN fellow? The one with those wretched cigars. He runs a shop too, no?"

"Kirby? Yes, but I haven't spoken with him in years. Can't just spring something like that outta the blue. That's not how business works. First I'd need to —"

A foot stomped. "Jack, shut up! Just shut up, you stupid fat fool! ShutUpShutUpShutUp! Please just don't say anything! You're a piece of garbage working in a garbage industry! Dunno why I ever expected more! Maybe I'm the REAL fool here! Maybe mother was right all along! Maybe I just shoulda listened!"

Hurling needles & yarn, Dot fled the room, a shower-tap roaring seconds later. Though a chance hadn't surfaced to raise the automat-confab, perhaps it was all for the best.

**WALLY GOOD SQUINTED** as his wife roamed the oneroomer, screaming in abject pain — wheeling about, hollering Teutonic, flesh rippling in delicate waves. The milk of a sunken left eye beamed pink incandescence.

"SWINE! SWINE! TOLD YOU NOT TO PUT IT THERE! HAVE YOU NO IDEA HOW MUCH THIS HURTS? I SHOULD SHOOT YOU! I SHOULD PUT

A HOLE RIGHT IN THE SIDE OF YOUR HEAD!"

Likewise bare, he lit a Camel, savoring the tingle, exhaling clouds as hands reached forwards. Inhaling deep, Tatiana blew a stream back. Chuckling, Wally Good palmed north — as if nipples aped tiny revolvers. "Sorry, Killer...didn't mean it. Some on your chin there too." Kneeling bedside, Tatiana smiled as curls were caressed.

They'd met in Frankfurt, where he'd been stationed postwar; an awful place, but still an improvement over Hokkaido's aboriginal lumps.

She rubbed lean shoulders. Pecked a thin neck.

"So, you start new job tomorrow?"

Wally Good squinted. He squinted most always, even whilst looking at nothing. "Please, liebling...no troubles this time. We need us that money real bad."

A grin fractured a forehead innumerable ways.

Twenty seven could've passed for fifty.

"Babe, any that whisky left?"

Tatiana retrieved a depleted pint. Inhaling dregs, Wally Good clapped then rubbed palms. "Don't worry, ain't gonna blow this. This is the big time. THE APPARITION. Dignity, class, yoddayodda..."

Standing, lobbing the empty aside, he donned tattered BVDs. "Wally — no! Where you go at so late?"

Crossing the room, rotating the switch of a clamped gooseneck, he slid a thin brush from a crammed jar. Licking, squinting — he smoothed sable strands betwixt a left pointer and thumb. "Calm down, ain't goin' nowhere. Gotta finish this story by the AM so I can drop it off on the way over to Meiser's."

"But Wally — you need sleep!"

"Ain't YOU the one gripin' 'bout dough? Gotta come from somewheres! If I start to fizz, I'll pop a bennie..."

A round face pouted & moaned.

"Fin in my wallet. Run down to the corner and get us more smokes. Grab another bottle there too."

"BUT WALLY — I'M NOT DRESSED!"

"Just toss on your robe! Jerkwater Central — not Gramercy Park! Think anyone here cares if
your hair's done or not?"

As his wife rose, Wally Good noted myriad rumpcraters. A veritable lunar-surface.

"Chopchop! This machine runs best on whisky!"

Seconds later, upon the door's slam, he powered a bakelite cube — spinning a dial back-and-forth before settling upon Webb Pierce's SLOWLY. Leaning back atop an overturned bucket, he squinted and smiled then sighed. Rejarring the brush, he lifted a woebegone Kay, strumming along best as he could. He saw a calico rug in front of a hearth near Collier's burning for warmth. An oaken Airline blared Jimmie Rodgers as a small boy illustratively scrawled. A mother bound stacked leaves with a Singer. A father rent labors to shreds.

Still strumming, Wally Good squinted at the page tacked to his table. A rocketsoaper full of Raymond swipes and Jane Russell bosoms. Boring...forgettable... but, as usual, heartdeluged. Everything was crisp. Cross-hatched. Craftinted. But it was the backgrounds that imbued bristol with life. Obsessively detailed, beyond convention, every inch of each tiny panel crammed with wires, spokes, stars, shadows, gears, comets & gleams. Wally Good often wondered why he pushed throwaway elements to such extremes. It certainly didn't increase his wages; nearly every other artist got by fine on dots-and-dashes alone. He wondered if anyone ever noticed his efforts.

What would a headshrinker make of it?

Another Camel was lit. Smoke diffused the page.

He studied a sink's draped knickers & bras. For a dame who claimed to care naught about clothes, Tots was awfully particular. Atop a girdle, a cockroach's antennae groped like a blind man searching for an old john's overhead-chain.

**WILL MEISER ARRIVED AT WORK** just before seven. Save for a large horsefly that seemed to have appeared from nowhere, the studio was lifedevoid.

The stentorian buzz irked to no end.

He wondered how on Earth a fly had made it all the way to November. Perhaps it was some strain of atomic-mutant? A tiny harbinger of God?

Neither theory was less distasteful.

Swatting the insect out of his office, he slammed the glass door — birthing a hundred webbed hairlines. Surveying the fractures, a bald dome quaked.

Uh-huh. Yup. Perfect.

Joints flaring, he collapsed to a chair,. Despite being amongst the youngest of his own staff, he was already a virtual Methuselah.

He'd been Bronxreared by immigrants.

In Vienna, Papa had been a professor at the Akademie der bildenden Künste Wien — Mama, a tutor of concert pianists. Here, they'd painted signs & sewed vests respectively.

Will had shown an early propensity for

draftsmanship upon Highbridge-sidewalks, specializing in compromised nudes. By the time he'd reached DeWitt Clinton, he'd won over a dozen regional-contests. He was going to be a famous painter, the man his father SHOULD have been! When the School of Music & Art opened on Midtown's East Side, young Will transferred immediately — there, talents continued to blossom.

One fateful day, Harold Gray visited to lecture the student-body. It wasn't the Great Man's rousing words that inspired Will Meiser's ambitions, but the chauffeured Duesenberg he'd arrived in.

Though Papa decried the funnies as a harebrained endeavor — suggesting Will stick tightly to nudes — an eight-dollar cheque from LIBERTY quickly reversed these opinions. In short order, Will discovered there was even more gelt to be verdient by peddling the toil of others. Five years' passage found him running the largest sweatshop within the fledgling comic book industry — a staff of thirty churning out thousands of pages, both for his own imprint and those of rivals.

1938 brought Superman and a booming public-demand. By age twenty two, Meiser had purchased his parents a three-story home, married his highschool sweetheart, and traveled to Paris, Athens & Macao. His closet housed a rackful of Brooks suits, Hermes ties, Borsalinos in twenty grey shades.

He'd once even shown Mayor O'Dwyer the joys of a Passover-seder. From virtually any angle — it was hard to argue that Will Meiser was not a true American Success.

Then came his recent woes.

They'd crept-up in nearimpalpable wisps.

Piddling diatribes denouncing comics as poison had begun appearing several years prior — efforts largely relegated to backends of rags few took serious. RED-BOOK. THE LADIES HOME JOURNAL. Soon, however, when shrewd editors recognized fat tubs of milk, serious periodicals commenced similar tomes. TIME. NEWSWEEK. THE AMERICAN MERCURY. THE KANSAS CITY STAR had even run a Lipstick Killer op-ed in which the psychopath heaped praised upon BULLETMAN & BLACK TERROR.

Now a stranger had phoned Will Meiser at home.

A government man — claiming to represent something called the Senate Subcommittee on Juvenile Delinquency. The bald man hadn't much liked that sound. He'd quietly requested the stranger ring again at his office; the last thing he needed was poor Ann worrying any more than she already had. He'd even journeyed nextdoor to consult his father. Alas, Papa's help had proven somewhat anemic.

"So, Mister Bigshot needs his poor father after all? Imagine that! Well, it don't take no Einstein to figure out this one! You wanna get blacklisted and go broke? You want no more fancy cars? No more gold watches? No more golfygolfy with the little stick? No more pheasant under the glass? Maybe some jail

even? And...for what? PROGRESS, Wilhelm!
Progress is the path of the true American!
Sentimentality is the path of the schmen-
drick! Which are you? That, YOU must decide!
And that...THAT is my advice for you, my son...
Mister Bigshot! Now, you will kindly excuse
me! BOXING FROM EASTERN PARKWAY is
on and I must see this Maxim geschlagen!"

He glanced at a wall's ukeleleshaped clock — its hum
aped that of the fly. He pondered rising, fleeing the
office, and never-ever returning. He wondered what
that'd be like. Mexico perhaps? Be another Sidney
Franklin? Already got the heroic jaw. Morocco?
He'd pined to see Tangier ever since THE SHELTER-
ING SKY. He wondered if William Heirens liked Paul
Bowles too, then decided he probably did.

**THE PHONE CLANGED** at precisely eight.

Patiently allowing the G-Man's spiel to unwind, pay-
ing only the scantest attention, the bald man recited a
pithy response composed on the morning's train in.

"Sir, I share your concerns on this matter.
While I've always striven to keep my books
wholesome & free of corrupt morals, there
are some financially-motivated, less-scrupu-
lous publishers who, unfortunately,
do not share this stance."

Upon the investigator's inquiry as to whom Meiser
might specifically refer, to whom he might finger with
the strongest conviction, his response took all of two
seconds. "Welp...Millard G. Gaines for one."

**THE HUSKY MAN** hunched by his desk rolling a small amber bottle. Tortoise bifocals enlarging type did nothing to quell mounting confusion. Lifting the vessel up to an ear, he shook thrice then lobbed. Landing atop a naugahyde couch, the bottle rattled & bounced. He punched the red button of a telephone the color of storebought keylime. "Vera?"

"Mister Gaines?"

"Vera, y'ever hear of 'Dexedrine'?"

"No sir — sounds like a drug or something. That it? Some kinda drug? A medicine?"

"Nevermind."

Blazing a smoke, Millard Gaines lifted Weejuns atop a desk teeming mounds of inked bristol. The remaining office was equally cluttered; a carpet ashlousy studded with nuts; wallpanels barristerchoked. Even a lowhung ceiling's asbestos was abysmally Zeppelin-mobbed. Running soft fingers through a black flattop, the husky man held a drag for ten seconds. Slowly exhaling, lowering shoes, he once again seized the phone — stabbing the first of four yellow buttons that immediately trailed their red chief.

"Yeah?"

"Feldberg?"

"YEAH?"

"Lissen...doc gave me something called Dexedrine..."

"Yeah?"

"Know anything about it?"

"Yeah."

"Well...what the fuck is it then?"

"It's diet pills. Like bennies, but for rich Jew housewives. Why for he give ya that? 'Cause yer so fuckin' fat?"

"So...it's what? A happy pill? That whatcha mean?"

"Yeah, that's what they say — but I'm the wrong guy to ask...y'know I don't touch that crap. Hear some of the boys use it when they got a tight deadline..."

"Well, maybe try it — just read your last script!"

Gaines chuckled as the phone clicked. Rising, circumnavigating trash. he retrieved a bottle lodged within couchdepths. Uncorking, shaking loose tablets, he glanced towards a cooler and cursed.

**A HASTY FORAGE** through an elephant's foot proved fruitful when chrome gleamed amidst umbrellas & swords. Pulling a slug, Millard Gaines WOWed before involuntarily dropping flasked rye.

He examined the small bottle once more — this time with extra precaution. TAKE ONE TABLET WITH FOOD EVERY SIX HOURS. Grunting, scanning, lifting tin capsized — the husky man crunched a palm of Utzdregs. Again he pondered the elephant's foot. Shorn from an albino longago pink, the limb now stood jaundiced with slime. His father had slain the beast back in '37. Cotridden a mile behind, the shots had rung Millard Gaines' young ears through a buffer of malarian haze. Rushing deskwards, warm & spry, again he grasped and harpooned.

"Yeah?"

"Okay...got a new idea for HALL OF DISGRACE!"

"Yeah?"

"Take this down! So there's this rich guy, see? Mean as fuck! Real ornery cocksucker! Always tellin' his son he's not good enough...at anything...that he's just a hunk of fat garbage! Anyhow, so one fateful day, this old man…this ornery cocksucker…he forces the poor schlub onna safari…"

**WALLY GOOD TRAVERSED** the frontdoor — a pasteboard folder within his left crook & the Kay right shoulderslung; the guitar's strap was wrought from the same fuzzed twine keeping his samples bound.

Jack Coal, draining the cooler, beamed eyes boggled and chary. "Judas Priest — what the heck's that? Wanna tell him to get lost or should I?"

"Y-y-y-y-you b-b-b-better d-do it, J-J-J-Jack — n-n-n-no-b-b-b-body l-l-l-l-listens t-t-to m-me anymore!"

Bleary eyes beamed mortified.

"But Bert…I listen to you…am I a nobody too?"

"N-n-no, J-J-Jack! Th-that's n-n-not w-what I m-m-meant t'all! Y-y-y-you…you're a s-s-SOME-b-body!"

Straightening posture as best he could, Jack Coal braced for impact; he enjoyed informing greenhorns there was simply no work to be had. He'd assumed his stance, pointer aloft, when Meiser broke free from his room — blazing past tables, puffing smoke like a loco, tweed limb fully outstretched.

"WallyWallyWally! Good to seeya, lad! CmonCmonCmon — followfollow! Howsabout we just shoot us some breeze before we getcha all settled?"

Buzzing Jack Coal, the bald man paused.

"Oh, Jackie! How's that wrap comin'?"

A mouth gaped back nonplussed.

"Again, nothin' TOO gruesome…just sweet & kind… maybe a little bit sad! Like I said — you just do you!"

Wally Good trailed Meiser officebound.

The newcomer hadn't even nodded hello.

"J-J-Jack? Th-th-th-th-that's the r-r-r-ringer? H-h-h-h-h-he looks l-like a-a-a de-de-de-de-de-delin-que-que-quent! A r-r-real j-j-jay d-d-d-dee!"

Ignoring his chum, Jack Coal trembled, too disgusted for words. Angry too. And hungry again. A pocket-swipe yielded Lifesavers. Lipslapping three, the stub was thrust left. "N-n-none for m-m-me, th-th-thanks! I-I-I-I-I'm w-way b-b-bey-y-y-yond s-s-s-s-saving!"

**BREAK EXPIRED,** a penciled splash was surveyed.
THE BUCKETS OF TEARS
CRIED OVER SPILT BEERS!
Lifting a glob of grey rubber, he grated it all away.
After several curt false-starts, full sketching resumed, dropshadows replacing faint cursive.
THE BEASTLY BITCH'S
BARREL OF BOHEMIAN BARF!
Glancing up, peering through Meiser's scarred pane — he woolgathered the convo within.

"So, Wally, my boy...tell me about the para-troops. What was it all REALLY like? Didja ever jerkoff midjump? How hard would your penis actually get in that one-piece? If the an-swer's too complex for words, feel free to whip it right out and give me a physical demo!"

"Well, Mister Meiser sir! Being a paratrooper was fabulous! Just fabulous! But instead of telling you, why don't I just play you a ballad I've written about it? HERE...I'll accompany myself on this hobo guitar I've inexplicably brought to a place of business!"

A sudden blur severed insight.
"J-J-J-J-Jack. D-d-did y-y-y-y-you w-w-w-watch

G-G-G-G-G-Godfrey last n-n-night? Th-th-th-th-th-that f-f-f-fellow o-on it l-l-l-l-looked j-j-j-j-just l-l-like y-y-y-you! Br-br-br-br-br-br-br-br…"

Jack Coal wheeled away, unable to stand his friend's stutter. He glanced back down to his table.

"…br-br-br-br-br…"

If only he could dive right into that page.

"BRUBECK!"

Testicles knotted & throbbed.

**DOT'S CIVILITY REMAINED ICY** at best as she awaited Elastic Man's hand-off. Although Jack Coal had made a few cursory gestures, the paramount moment to broker a deal had yet to make itself known.

This was a subject that demanded finesse and Meiser had been uncharacteristically jumpy. Twice within the past week alone, Jack Coal had espied sticky red hankies piled atop the bald man's blotter.

Made perfect sense the jerk would get ulcers — that young turk's hiring was surely proving a catastrophic mistake. Whose bile WOULDN'T rile over that?

He'd broach things again when conditions improved. Ol' man Coal wouldn't let his darling down…

Nuh-uh…simply won't do!

**THAT NIGHT HE DREAMT** back to his nineteenth year. NEW CASTLE. AMERICAN CAN.

Dot's hair was slick & bobbed.

Cheeks — rosy & plush.

A swelling belly soon gave way to kittens which Jack Coal drowned in the Shenango. Lacking a sack, he dunked them one at a time while his beloved basked atop the bank's mud. When a bearded catfish snagged a stray floater — Jack Coal's groping right arm elongated ten yards in pursuit.

**AWAKENING AT TWO**, he rolled to face Dot, who was wheezing in twelve distinct notes. Returning to sleep proved difficult — following nine hundred & six impotent sheep, Jack Coal fled to the bathroom.

Perched on the toilet, he mulled Dot's words.

Perhaps there was something to them?

Perhaps Meiser WOULD let him have Elastic Man gratis? After all, what use could he have for a property he was scrapping anyway? A property he'd never seemed to give two licks about?

Had he ever marketed Elastic Man? Had he ever even tried? Perhaps things would be DIFFERENT if so!

There were Superman cartoons. Superman serials. Superman cereals. Superman dolls. Superman paddleballs. Superman diapers. Superman window-wipers. Jack Coal had once even spotted a Negro child fondling a yellow packet of Supercigarettes. The Batman was everywhere. Captain Marvel and Spy Smasher too. Even Angrygirl — a character with virtually no fans — had been merchandised to her lackluster hilt.

But ELASTIC MAN? NOTHING! Zilch!

No shirt-transfers! No wristwatches!

Not even a giveaway whistle...

He fumed on the toilet, mind racing, livid at the thought of untapped potential. Elastic Man was special! He deserved better than this! Even amongst a flood of clichés, he remained supremely unique! He was boneless — devoid of all skin, blood, pus & nails — his makeup entirely rubber! He could stretch for miles and never break! Alter his appearance to resemble anybody or -thing he chose! He could be a rockingchair, Grandma Moses, a sarcophagus, a Socialist, a grand piano, Mel Ott, even a holy bible! He could be male, female, tall, short, adult, child, or llama! He could neither be shot nor stabbed nor maimed nor frozen nor shredded nor chopped nor burned!

It'd all been tried before!

The feature was unique in other ways too.

Elastic Man was no run-of-the-mill alien, mystical orphan, or vengeful playboy. Here was a legitimate EVERYMAN — a wretched criminal gifted a chance at redemption by some strange twist of Fate.

EVERYBODY wanted a second-chance!

People could RELATE to the concept!

Even his sidekick Fuzzy Finks was special. He too was an ex-hood; not some implausible, barelegged preteen. Scrotum-cheeked, imbecilic, utterly self-absorbed — Fuzzy's lone supernatural power was the ability to instantaneously depress. Will Meiser had particularly lauded Jack Coal upon Finks' introduction, referring to the character as:

"A brutalfully sublime form of comic-relief."

And now the dumb kike wanted to gum the works!

Maybe Dot's right! Maybe Hyman & Kirby WOULD take on his boy for the win! Inhaling deeply, clenching lids, Jack Coal pondered Kirby and sighed.

**THOUGH NO MORE** than five four in spectator lifts, Zach Kirby projected quite huge. Doublebreasteds sporting chalkstripes & pads — obscenely brimmed Knox Twenties — penile double-coronas.

While he was wellregarded by industry peers, his

choppy work diametrically opposed Will Meiser's. His
heroes were stiff & ogrefaced. His women resembled
blonde Chinamen. Nonetheless, despite all logic and
reason, there was a ferocious kineticism to Kirby's
panels that no other cartoonist could touch.

Jack Coal farted and shat simultaneously.

How many hours had he pored over those lurid
splashes attempting to decipher their magic?

He'd last lain eyes upon the little man himself in a
Great Jones boxcar-diner. As he strained to recall the
'48 gather, memories hailed down in soft blotches...

Spoons clanked mugs.

Bacon hissed.

Kirby smirked as Jack Coal's tale unraveled.

He hailed from PA — just shy of Ohio — where
his father had kept a small store. He had a
sheepdog — Ralph — and his very best friend
was his brother.

Tyrone had been named after an uncle
who'd quit life a day past brakeman-retire-
ment. He'd simply donned his Sunday best
then lain across the tracks at dawn. As his
only good clothes had been utterly wrecked,
Uncle Ty was buried in mottled pink woolens.
At the wake, his brother had whisped:

'Figure he's in three pieces or five?'

He'd told Zach Kirby about the summer
he'd rode a Schwinn to LA just to see what
the tarpits looked like himself. "Nine weeks it
took! Even wrote-up a story that BOYS LIFE
bought! In fact, it was my very first sale!"

Kirby'd stared back, masticating — his focus

imbuing discomfort. "Yeah? And?"

"And what, Zach?"

"Well...and what'd ya think of California?"

"Why, it was the most beautiful place I'd ever seen! Heaven on Earth! Ever been to San Diego, Zach? Ever smelled an orange grove's sweet waft in the morning?"

Rending wheat toast in twain, the little man shook a broad head.

"Can't say I have, Jack. Can't say I have. Okay — so then, you get back East. Then what?"

"And then...then I finished highschool...married Dot senior-year...though we kept it hush-hush at first."

"Didn't tell nobody? Not even your folks?"

"Nope, ESPECIALLY not them...I didn't even tell Tyrone! Heck, didn't even tell Ralphie! Figured he might growl something about it in his sleep!"

Sopping grease, the little man chuckled.

"That's rich! Gotta remember that one..."

Although Jack Coal had reciprocally grinned — inside, he'd seethed at the patronization of a racial inferior.

"So, Jack, why was that? Why for didja hafta keep mum?"

"Well...y'see...Dorothy...she was with child..."

Kirby grunted — gulping more hash.

"Knocked-up, huh? Know how that is, brother. So the kid...must be 'bout twenty now, huh? He in college? The service? Or wait, maybe it's a girl. Got two of 'em myself. Oh hey! Hey doll! Can we get us some Tabasco here?"

Receiving a tiny red bottle, Kirby slapped at its heel with vigor — dousing potatoes, onions, and curled bovine scabs with dollops viscous & crimson. Jack Coal studied his own plate.

Grits resembled babyfood.

"We...um...we lost the child. Dot's been unable to conceive ever since..."

Though Kirby's frown was swift & sincere, Jack Coal again ragewelled. He sought no pity from squat trolls.

"Aw geez...that's a shame, Jack. Real tough break. But what then? Got hitched then what?"

"Then I went to work for American Can."

"What's that? Like a can factory or something?"

"Yes, a can factory."

Grunting and nodding, Kirby continued to shovel forkfuls of hash — Jack Coal wondered how such a primitive little monkey could possess so much talent. "And you? From whence did you sprout, Zach?"

Not even bothering to glance up from his trough, the little man spoke in guttural, food-muddly bursts. "Not too far from here. Lower East. Orchard & Delancey. Weren't easy, Jack. No sir...weren't..."

Belching loudly, coffeeswishing shards loose, Kirby again angled his fork and bore down.

"No sir. Mean, you been down there...right? You know what it's like — and me bein' such a shrimp and all — sink-or-swim, all'a damn time. Kill-or-be-killed, y'know? Every day, another scrap! Every day, a fight to survive, see?"

Jack Coal chuckled, internally, visualizing an even tinier Zach Kirby battling neighborhood toughs in patched corduroy knickers. The scene had all the exaggerated dynamicism of a CAPTAIN BLAMMO special.

At least, he thought he'd been chuckling internally. "Somethin' funny, Jack?"

Catching himself, tapping a pane, Jack Coal breathed a sigh of relief as Kirby faced the opposing sidewalk. A fat man in lavender was attempting to gather a toy poodle's disproportionately large feces. Apparently locked within bent-posture, the fat man shook whilst struggling to stand, teetering upon a face-first collapse. Perched by its efforts, the immaculately-groomed, minuscule dog bobbled a long loping tongue.

It appeared to enjoy its master's distress.

Kirby's chews slowed with due focus.

"Hah! Yeah, I see. The fat fuck! Well, anyway, yeah...so I grew up. Then Uncle Sam came knockin'..."

Jack Coal turned away from the poodle, which he could've sworn had just winked and blown kisses.

"Oh, yes — you were in Will's outfit, assigned to STARS & STRIPES, correct? Seem to recall him mentioning so..."

Scraping teeth with a right nail, the little man sucked a fingertip clean. "For a minute — 'til I slugged a lippy punk louie."

"And then?"

"Then...infantry. Hearda the Bulge?"

"Yes, of course."

The little man surveyed his plate as if it contained a roadmap. "Gotta tellya, Jack. What you said about seein' the world on that bike-ride...I can relate! Seen a lotta things over there! Things no fella should ever hafta see! Seen men burnt to death right next to me! Watched the skin bubble up on a guy's forehead and his eyeballs swell up and pop just like they was two marbles! Seen this kraut with both his mitts blown clear-off layin' in the mud, screamin' like a little baby! Just like a hungry tyke in its crib! I killed him..."

A milky infant wearing an oversized helmet smiled inside the brain of Jack Coal.

He swallowed more grits.

"Shoot him in the head?"

The little man smirked.

"Nah, Jack. Like I said, this was a kraut. Woulda been too good for him..."

Shoveling the last of his hash, Kirby gargled with coffee.

"Emptied·a full magazine all over his balls..."

Nodding, Jack Coal attempted to smile.

"Well, it certainly sounds like this fellow deserved it. I mean, Nazis — after all they'd done to your people..."

"No, no, that ain't right, Jack! Never said he was no Nazi! Most of them krauts wasn't Nazis. Just soldiers like us. Think maybe I was just havin' a bad day..."

Jack Coal rubbed at his chin. "I see."

"Things I seen in the cathouses over there was even worse — pussies with sores fatter'n cow's eyes!"

A passing waitress sent a check fluttering onto the splashed linoleum. Withdrawing a long eelskin billfold, Zach Kirby waved Jack Coal off. "And what was your war like?"

Jack Coal swirled fulvous yolk tiers throughout his languishing grits.

"Oh. Wasn't quite as glamorous."

Grunting again, Kirby yanked loose five leaves of napkin and rubbed at his catfishy lips. "Oh, mean you was a P.O.W. or somethin'? E.T.O. or Pacific? "

"No, no. None of that. I was declared unfit for service."

Cringing upon a boorish guffaw, Jack Coal pondered a shaker's heavy cutglass.

"Wha? C'mon, big strappin' mug like yourself? Who'd a thunk it? What wuzzit? Bum ticker? Mastoiditis? Incurable dandruff?"

Would his blood run Red, White & Blue?

"No. Nothing like that. There was just...a... a misunderstanding."

"HAHAHAHA! Tell 'em you was a FAIRY or somethin'? Ah, Jack, old bean, that's rich! You break me up!"

Jack Coal tilted his head. If war was Hell, discussing it was Hell's sub-basement.

"Well, no. Not quite that. It was on account of confessing to the board that I was guilty of being a cartoonist."

"WHA?"

"But cartoonist wasn't specific enough for them. They pressed me. So...told them I was in the comic books."

"Yeah? So what? When I told 'em I created Captain Blammo, they practically named me general right onna spot!"

"Well, then perhaps I should've claimed to be your assistant. Anyhow, after I'd explained to the fellows that I drew Elastic Man, they held a little pow-wow in the back. When they'd finished, the recruiting-officer — that is, at least, the sergeant in charge — pulled me aside for some more questions."

"Questions like what?"

"Well...rather embarrassing, troublesome questions..."

"Yeah? Like what? What'd they ask?"

"First he asked me if I'd had a good relationship with my father. I said, 'Yes, of course,' but he just frowned. Then he waved one of the younger fellows over and asked him to repeat something."

"Repeat what?"

"Please Zach — I'm getting to that. So, he asked this young man, who was apparently some sort of funnies-enthusiast, to share his personal-take on Elastic Man."

"And the kid says what?"

"Something to the effect of: 'Well, sir, he's a convicted felon who's gained the power to become either gender and traverses the world battling ne'er-do-wells with his flamboyant male companion, also an ex-con.' Then the older officer looked me over, rather stern I might add, and asked if this was an accurate assessment."

"To which you said?"

"Well, Zach, I couldn't just lie, could I? These were GOVERNMENT men! While this young man's synopsis wouldn't quite match the way I'D describe the feature — there's obviously far more to it than that — none of what he'd said had been...technically...inaccurate..."

"So then what?"

"Then...then they asked me if Elastic Man was...a...a deviant..."

"So, like a fruit, right? A fairy?"

"Those weren't the words they used, Zach. They merely said 'DEVIANT'."

"To which you answered?"

"Zach...seriously — what COULD I say? How could I, in good conscience, not admit that Elastic Man was indeed some form of deviant, albeit of the reformed variety? He IS, after all, a spawn of the underworld."

"And then they said?"

"Then...they inquired as to if I too was... a deviant."

"And?"

"I said: 'No, don't think so. But you're certainly welcome to ask my wife.'"

"Then they did what?"

"Then...then they phoned Dot."

"Who says what?"

"Well, I'm not quite certain. Never felt it pertinent to ask..."

Leaning back in the booth, Kirby smirked with a bricolage of amusement, pity & contempt. A cigar removed from a breastpocket was guillotined with a chipped yellow tooth. A matchstrike ushered heavy blue smoke that rested on air as if shelved.

"Well, Jack...guess some of us hadda deliver the milk."

A hairnetted redhead in a neighboring booth tapped the little man's shoulder and scowled.

"Gee whiz, mister — that thing stinks like Old Nick! Mind takin' it outside so us gals can dine here in peace?"

Ignoring the woman, Kirby crushed a crisp sawbuck and lobbed it behind his right shoulder. Landing atop a splitpea pool, the bill floated like a frosty crouton.

**AS THE FAT MAN LEANED** against Lafayette bricks, passersby glared with mocking, supercilious eyes. He shivered.

This Eastern air was just too darn cold!

What about California?

He gazed down upon a tiny poodle whose wheeze deadrang a cackle. Even SHE seemed to regard him derisively, having destroyed his five best toupées the night prior. As the pair began to once again amble, the fat man yanked a Tyrolean tighter.

Turning west onto Bleecker, towards Washington Square, the poodle's gait amplified. While the fat man struggled to keep pace with his dog, she repeatedly found herself choking. Despite this annoyance, she refused to slow down. If one was doomed to be publicly tethered, then one should at least be seen as coxswain.

The little poodle missed the other fat man dearly. The one with the yellow hair that those strange dark creatures had carted-off several moons back.

He'd never failed to brush her wires nightly.

The fat man missed the other fat man too.

Life wasn't fair.  This had been doubly-so for his beloved Butch — a beautiful, shining gem.

A prince! Gentle as a lamb!

All he'd ever wanted to do was strum his mandolin and make children happy...

Who dies from a flybite's infection?

It just doesn't make any sense!

The pair paused by a blind violinist playing 'BLU-TROTE ROSEN' to a turnout of none. The fat man smiled — Butchie adored that song — but the poodle relentlessly tugged. There were rats to chase.

As the fat man was dragged forcibly off, silver was lobbed atop velvet.

Intaking wafts of floral cologne, the blind man bowed in approval. "Grazie signora."

**SETTLING ATOP A WORN BENCH,** the fat man released his poodle to a lawn anemic & butty. While unleashing one's dog within public-parks was against ordinance — thus risking citation or censure — the fat man could envision no viable alternative. If Stella was denied even ONE noonday-romp, she was liable to become spiteful for weeks. And a ticket, at worst, simply meant someone new to pass a few moments with. Money was no longer a concern — Butchie had left a him a prosperous chocolatery.

· If only there was someone to share it with!

Glancing up, he pondered a chambray sky rife with static white clouds. One resembled James K. Polk. Another, a cake left out in the rain.

Still another aped a titanic horsefly.

How strange!

Lowering chins, the fat man chuckled.

Before him, mackinawswathed, a black boy beamed a wide smile. Warmth-deluged, the fat man grinned back. As frightening as they were fullgrown, few things in life pleased him more than lilliputian Negroes. "Well, hello there! Aren't you something?"

The smiling black child nodded. "Hullo."

"So then, young man — what might your name be?"

"Lester."

"Why...LESTER! How dignified! Knew another Lester once! Very strong fellow! He was in the Marine Corps. He was...killed...by a German...in Flanders..."

While the fat man granted Lester ample time to react — the black child merely stared.

"A shame it was. A real darn shame. Tragic. So hand-some, so gallant. Cut down in his prime...just like a beautiful orchid..."

Lester, still beaming, nodded.

"That's nice."

Seepage was dabbed from a left eye.

"Yes. He was rather nice."

A peach fingertip jabbed towards the lawn.

"Mista, do that be your dog there yonda?"

Craning, the fat man shuddered. Stella was rolling in chalky brown dust, a thrashing grey rat in her mouth. Frantic, piercing, nearhuman screams ceased with a crisp wet pop.

"Yep, that's my dog."

"Well, what he be doin' then?"

"She...she likes to hunt rats."

"Ain'tcha got you no money fo' no dogvictuals?"

"Oh, yes — plenty! And she gets PLENTY of food! The expensive brands too! Only the best! Very refined tastes, understand, on account of she's French!"

"But...then...then why fo' he be doin' that?"

Shrugging dolorous, the fat man sighed.

"Some people...some things...are just born to kill, I guess. Some things are lovers. Some are killers. And some...some things are both..."

As the black child's smile spread everbroader, the fat man's lips wrenched likewise. Lester's grin was an infectious disease. "Mista?"

"Yes?"

"Can I have a quarta?"

Pocketfishing, the fat man paused. "Well, Lester, it's your lucky day! I've already donated my spare-change to the arts, so you're going to receive a whole dollar!"

Withdrawing a sheaf clipped by a gold B, the fat man

fretted as leaves unfurled.

"Oh Lester...sorry. So very sorry. No singles today —"

Beneath an arched Tyrolean brim, eyes covert glimpsed a frown's birth.

"— so you'll just have to accept ten dollars instead!"

**WATCHING THE BLACK CHILD** gallop past a bronze Garibaldi, the fat man leaned forwards and clapped. Oh what fun he'll have the next few days — licorice twists & cowboy pictures!

Behind him, Stella disemboweled her prey whilst pigeons warred over flecks of viscera.

**SKULKING BEHIND** Wally Good's table, Jack Coal watched 'THE APPARITIONAUT' take form.

He smirked. By the newcomer's boots, right in plain sight, a scrapbook broadcast glued Fosters.

Jack Coal had never swiped a thing in his life!

Professionals didn't steal!

Nor did they wield blue pencils!

Pity oozed from glands; not just for Wally — but also for poor ulcerated Will Meiser. This callow youth was infecting his baby with a taint from which it would never recover!

"So...hear you like that Zip-A-Tone bunk, huh? Not me! Too nitpicky, I say! All that tracing & cutting..."

Pausing midsketch, Wally Good craned rear and squinted. "Saves time. Creates consistency."

Arms shrugged.

"Well call me old-fashioned but I prefer just DRAW-ING the lines! That's how Will likes it done too..."

Nodding, Wally Good turned.

"Name's Coal, by the way. Draw ELASTIC MAN. Occupy that table right there."

Halting again, Wally Good shot air through nostrils.
"Yeah? Heard you was here.
Always liked your stuff."
"So...what's the ol' gitbox for? Sidebusking for beers?"
"Rehearsin' tonight with some fellas
downtown. That alright by you?"
"Well...just glad to finally get some color up in here!"
Leaning forwards, Wally Good grunted and drew.
"So...kay then...welcome aboard!"
Loitering for two minutes further,
Jack Coal grasped his dismissal.

**SQUATTING ATOP MUNITION-CRATES,** Zach
Kirby gnawed a stump while he scrawled.
Another boring romance.
He was sick of love! SICK! Sick to death!
The studio was located within the musty basement of
Joe Hyman's Forest Hills home. Beside the little man's
feet, atop cement cracked, leadsmutty leaves begged
completion. While most pencilers finished two or
three pages per day, Zach Kirby averaged ten...some-
times as many as twelve. Far too much for Joe to ink
solo — the duo farmed-out this surplus.
Zach Kirby never thought at the board, the
work simply flowed like spilt water — as if
pencils arrived artloaded and all one need do
was scrape. While there was no logical expla-
nation for this to occur, the jinxfearful little
man never once questioned his source.
Joe Hyman descended unpainted pine toting a sheaf
of 16"x20" Strathmore. Handsome and a full foot tall-
er than Zach, he functioned as the partnership's face.
Scowling through smoke, swatting a horsefly, Kirby

spied Joe's load with contempt.

It was inkless.

A pencil was hurled towards a cinderblock-wall, in which it lodged & shivered.

"THE FUCK'S THAT?"

Joe Hyman shrugged as he lowered the pages unto a pile already teeming.

"Russo returned 'em. Said they stunk."

"WHA? The fuck's that? Who the fuck's he? Motherfuckin' Paulie Picasso? Joe, YOU TELL ME — do those pages stink? Since when does it MATTER what this crap looks like anyway? It's garbage for snotnosed punks & droolin' morons!"

The tall man chuckled.

"Now, now Zach m'boy...compose thyself! The work's swell! He meant that the pages LITERALLY stink!"

"Ah! Well, then it's YOUR fault, see? I mean — you wrote that bowl'a tripe!"

"Nonono, bubala. Literally means actually. He means the paper ACTUALLY stinks!"

"WHA? Stinks like what?"

"Cigars! C'mon...he's got a small place, works in his kitchen, says his wife just can't TAKE it no more..."

The little man shrugged. "Imagine that? Fat fuckin' greaseball smells like a fishmonger's cart and yet he can't stand him a little cigar! Can you imagine how bad his wife's QUEEFS must stink?"

Head aquake, Zach Kirby yanked the stump from his lips just as the fly alighted its cherry. Singed & flightless, Kirby shook the bug loose — his partner's heel sealed the job on the floor.

Hyman & Kirby were a team.

The little man continued to smolder. He didn't like forgiveness. Grudges were rungs to success.

"I mean, who ever hearda such things? Ginzo can't stand a little smoke? Says he was at Wake Island and CIGAR SMOKE bothers him? Tellin' ya, don't wash!"

The tall man shrugged as he leaned to inspect the fresh page crowding the table. "So his wife can't stand the smoke — whaddya want from me, baby? We'll find ya another inker! Say, some DISH you're workin' on there! Yassuh bossuh! Gonna ink this one myself..."

Thin lips smacked lusty approval. "How I LOVE me a dame in a tight sweater...yassuh boss...yes sir!"

Glancing down to the page, the little man sighed.

"Joe, gotta level here. Been thinkin' on this a long time. I wanna do things — different kinda things, see? Wanna do things that ask for ANSWERS! Things that DEMAND answers! Like, PHILOSOPHICAL shit, see? Ever since the war...I dunno...I just...I just SEE things differently! I mean, like, a GRANDER SCHEME or somethin'! Dunno...I mean...gotta be more to all this than just kissypoo shit! Right? See?"

The tall man eyed his partner perplexed.

"God...cheeses...not this again! Please — Zach — bubala! Baby! I DON'T see! I have absolutely NO IDEA what the fuck you keep goin' on about! You want answers? Answers to WHAT? Our sales are good! Great even! Not a lotta folks can say that right now! This teevee bushwah's killing almost everyone else! Gratitude! Thankfulness! Now THAT'S an answer!"

"Ah, well, yeah...I mean, I am! I AM thankful! But Joe...don't it ever eat at you too? Not even a little? You know...like life's questions? The deep shit? Joe, don'tcha know what I mean? Like, why the fuck are we here? What the fuck's it all about? Where are we goin' and what will it fuckin' cost? Didn't the war change you none at all?"

Smirking, Joe Hyman saluted.

"United States Coast Guard, remember?"

"Yeah, but don'tcha ever sit up at night and ponder things on, like, a more GALACTIC scale? Don'tcha ever wonder 'bout things that HAVE BEEN...and things that are TO COME?"

Placing fingertips at either temple, Joe Hyman bore down as he spieled. "Honestly, Zach...baby...hand-to-God...love ya like a brother...but no, I DON'T understand! When I sit up at night and wonder, it's about how in the blazes am I gonna pay for Seth's fuckin' school while Bessie keeps runnin' up rizik tabs at Gimbel's! THAT's what I fuckin' wonder about! You want the meaning of life...ask a rabbi or something!"

A right hand waved in disgust.

"No thank you, Joe! THROUGH with that hokum! Where they been? What they done? I been through WAR, Joe! Seen things! Really lived! Been thinkin', Joe! Been thinkin' a lot, see? Thinkin' we can really DO something here!"

"But do WHAT? You mean with the funnybooks?"

Zach Kirby leapt four feet in the air.

"YES! With the funnies! Only NOT-so-funny! Like, somethin' with real BIG LEAGUE meanin'!"

A door creaked at the top of the stairs.

Shrills pierced through its crack.

"Joe! Oh Joe!"

The tall man winced in pain.

"Yes, Bessie sweetheart? What is it, oh Dearest One?"

"JOE!!!"

"Oh...what is it, my bountifully bodacious bundle of buoyancy?"

"Joe! What're we gonna name this baby? It's almost time now and I still don't know what to tell Mama!"

Joe Hyman winked at his partner.

"Told ya, Honey! If it's a girl, then Tinkerbell! A boy — we call 'im Simon!"

"But...Simon?"

"That's the idea! SIMON HYMAN!"

The slammed door was insufficient to mask anguished sobs. Once again, Joe Hyman glanced down to the table, running a finger alongst the perimeter of a bosom defiantly erect. "Meaning, huh? Okay...I'm hep, Daddy-O! You mean like Mailer, right?"

Unwrapping a fresh corona, toothshearing its ass, Zach Kirby waved his cigar like a wand.

"Nah! Nah, not quite like that! But not too far off neither! Thinkin' more like THE FOUNTAINHEAD meets FRANKENSTEIN meets FLASH GORDON meets SIGMUND FREUD!"

Orbs rolling, Joe Hyman whistled through abundant saliva. "Yeah, Zach...kids are gonna love that...especially the pickaninnies...deeper the better for them!"

**RETURNING TO 88 PERRY,** scaling bowed stairs — Lester toted a sackful of booty from a hunchback's Sixth Ave newsstand.

He'd been sent North several months prior, following a mysterious blaze that'd immolated nine siblings & cousins. Fearing Beaufort a poor fit for her boy, Lester's mother had decreed his best chance for survival lurked within her eldest son's keep.

Cornell Humberto Jackson, possessor of a PhD from Morningside Heights, was the first of their kin to study beyond the third grade. Taking on a ward had proven challenging — Cornell had been rejected from eighty five teaching-positions thus far. Shunned even in Harlem — he was simply too dark for whites yet too erudite to mentor his own. Fortunately, he was amply tall and handsome enough to stir groins within the wellheeled & lonesome.

The scholar was in the kitchen ironing oxfords when Lester scampered towards the WC.

"Careful, LeeLee! Just had that suit in there laundered! Muss it and there WILL be consequences!"

Ignoring this caution, Lester slammed a door from which a grey herringbone hung reeking of naphtha & cedar. Though Lester did indeed feel love for his brother, his fussiness often triggered icepick-reveries. Extricating a moist Juicy Fruit glob, Lester buried it betwixt puffs of a hanky's silk blossom.

Standing atop the toilet's rim, lifting a crusty window, he took hold of a stringdangling can. Yanking back & forth, he cupped an ear then waited. Following an unacceptable span, jangling anew, Lester peered north.

A windowsprouting sallow mien rifled eldritch gibberish. "BADBOY! REAVEBOBBYARONE! GOWAYBADBOY! BOBBYNORIKEYNOMOLE!"

Chuckling, forcing the window shut, Lester set-out for the frontdoor. Passing Cornell on the way, a peace-offering was lobbed to the sink.

"And what might that be?"

"Milky Way, Mounds & Pall Malls."

Manicured eyebrows furrowed then eased.

"While I thank you very kindly for the munificence — how did you pay for all this hmmn?"

"Fat white man — me & him is good friends."

Fists-upon-hips, Cornell swiveled and clucked — gestures absorbed from their mother.

"LeeLee, really...a white man just GAVE it to you? Did he happen to be sleeping on a subway hmmn?"

"No! Dang — honest! He just a fat man in the park! On a bench! Waked! Toldja 'bout him befo'! He a nice ol' man! Know a dead Maureen too!"

"I see...and just what does this fat man on a bench ask you to DO for this money?"

"Nuthin'! HONEST, Corny! Just a nice ol' man! Got him a French dog that eat a rat fo' lunch every day!"

"Lester, I don't want you taking money from strange white men anymore! I don't approve — it's not right."

"WHY FO? YOU DO IT ALL'A DANG TIME!"

The door slammed.

Lifting his iron, Cornell sighed.

**ALREADY STOOP-PERCHED** by the time Lester arrived, Bob Fujitani was damp. Bob Fujitani was always damp. This syndrome struck Lester as strange.

"Why fo' you's all sweaty? Chinee folks don't sweat!"

"Because I'm bigboned! And I'm NOT Chinese — I'm Japanese! JAPAN! Different country! How many times do I have to explain this?"

Lester shrugged indifferently.

He neither knew nor cared.

**THE DUO PORED OVER A PILE** of fresh comics with the zeal of Cambridge tombraiders. Lester had carefully selected only the bloodiest titles.

CAVERN OF CRIME
AFRICAN WITCHCRAFT
WEIRD TALES OF DEATH & DISEASE

As a special concession to obsolete tastes, he'd even purchased one superhero book —

WONDER WOMAN

Though this strange obsession with a girl's feature went well beyond Lester's grasp, Bob Fujitani was his lone friend — as such, he simply ignored such flaws.

Splitting his treasure, tapping a panel, the Japanese boy leered ecstatically. "OH LESTER...LOOK!"

An evil man with Semitic features was hopelessly lariatsnared. However, the fiend was hardly miffed.

On the contrary — he was smiling.

"I LIKE IT WHEN SHE TIES PEOPLE UP!"

Noting a corduroy tent, pity deluged Lester's being.

**JACK COAL WAS ALERTED** to his wife's presence by the simultaneous shriek of ten stools.

Between kidgloves hovered the globe.

He studied her burden bewildered.

Two floating lumps kissed back.

"Darling, you'll need to return these please."

"But hon...whatever for?"

"Oh, they're just too darn loud! Can't seem to get ANYTHING done with all their incessant bumping about...it's getting so I can't hear myself think!"

Removing the orb from Dot's clutch, Jack Coal scanned the bullpen for suitable perches. Every stool

was manned — nary a table angled at less than forty degrees. Crossing the room to a far corner, he set
the bowl atop a radiator neighboring the dusty sill's
fly-graveyard. The fish smiled up at him sadly.

Turning around, Jack Coal was aghast to discover his
wife staring over Wally Good's shoulder. Scurrying
back, coiling a waist, he pretended to likewise admire a fullpage splash. Reflected within a rocketship's
window, The Apparition's grim mien loomed impotent
against the vastness of space.

Surveying fields gaseous, Jack Coal looked inwards
for some form of untapped strength.

He'd never thought it possible that a background
might overshadow a fore. It was improper.

Pretentious. Showoffy.

But somehow, it made him feel impotent too.

A glove cupped his left ear softly.

"Sweetheart...who is this man and why is he
working on THE APPARITION?"

"Ah, just some young punk."

"I'm certainly no expert...but is he not kinda
pretty darn good?"

Jack Coal scratched at his groin. "Alright, I guess."

Dot watched Wally's thin brush birth a meteortrail.
"Find a chance to call Kurtzstein yet?"

An aching head wagged slowly.

Pecking a cheek, hiding eyes, Dot's voice trembled as
she struggled to rebutton her coat. "Gosh, so smoky in
here! I'll never figure out how you survive!"

"Often wonder myself..."

Atop the radiator, in the far corner,
the globe bubbled over with steam.

**HE PEERED UP AT CLOUDS** jetty as soot, uncertain to blame God or Man's filth.

This was not Dick Steele's best day.

Jesus Cripes...talk about hangovers.
Need something to kill all this pain.

He visited a Chinese druggist for Paregoric.

Outside, cap shouldertossed, he downed the shebang in one swallow. Flipping the empty to a wire trashbin, he soldiered on — southwards, straight down .the Bowery.

Out from a shadow crept an oliveskinned beast, which bayed as it seized the small bottle. Lifting the vessel up to its tongue, a stubborn last drop was beat loose.

Mellowing with analgesia, Dick Steele studied hands as he stumbled. Nails caked brown.

Fuggit. Tomorrow — today will be yesterday.

**AT CHATHAM SQUARE,** a barber's loud awning hawked TATTOOS IN THE REAR!

Dick Steele eyed a window rife with sepia cards.

Each highlighted a tophatted gent engraving an Edwardian nude. Dried roses littered the platform beneath, winged cadavers sown betwixt; one even affixed with a thin streamer of a legend too pale to read.

Jesus Cripes. What kinda sickfuck glues tissue to some tiny, innocent fly?

**STAGGERING IN,** brushing past barbers, Dick Steele headed all the way to the back — where a shirtless mummy and a likewise bare sailor reeked of urine, Listerine & dried sweat.

He ogled the mummy for several dull moments before pegging the tophatted gent. Time's gap had been unkind.

Orbs sidewinding beneath a celluloid visor, the mummy winked as it pailwrung a browned sponge.

"Sit, m'boy! Sit on down! With ya right inna jiffy!"

Above a far stool hung a cracked pane rancid with flyspecks & scabs. Spitting-up glass, sleeve a'wipe, Dick Steele leaned forwards to read.

EAST COAST MECHANIC'S QUARTERLY
Spring, 1927
FROM A MASTER TATTOOIST
by Professor Chas. Wagner esq.

By way of introduction, I am Professor Charles Falstaff Wagner of New York City, U.S.A.

For some thirty years now, I have wielded a reputation as the world's leading practitioner of the ancient art of skin illustration. I am also the world's foremost historian and safe-keeper of the ancient art of skin illustration. In addition, I am the world's sole reputable producer and distributor of professional tattooing supplies and equipment.

The practice of skin illustration is not a modern phenomenon, but an ancient rite dating back in recorded human history over some three thousand years; though it has been noted by some anthropologists that it is quite possible Man first began decorating his body whilst still dwelling in caves.

Many of the world's best-known historical figures wore their tattooing quite proudly. It is a well known fact that the ancient Sumerians were quite adept at tattooing — a skill they passed on to the Vikings, who later gifted these secrets to the Hebrews. Portraits of King Solomon, rendered whilst the monarch still reigned, often depict him covered head-to-toe in beautiful engravings of a lurid,

floral motif. Alexander the Great was known to wear a
rose tattoo over his heart in honor of his beloved mother Olympias. Jesus Christ himself had many tattooings
inscribed within his divine flesh, most being recitations of
sacred Judean scripture & lore.

I myself have had the distinct honor of applying skin
illustrations atop the cream of the Earth's gentry – everyone from Presidents McKinley, Roosevelt & Wilson, to
Harold the great monarch of Sweden, to pugilist Jess 'The
Pottawatomie Giant' Willard. But I beg you not to think me
some snob. I am just as home tattooing a Times Square
'copper' as I was last year when visited by none other than
– that great diva herself – Lady Isadora Duncan. Indeed,
no other tattooist can factually claim to have provided the
full-body skin illustrations of every major 'fat lady' attrac-
tion within our vast Western Hemisphere.

In addition, I have been provided with a generous
retainer to remain the exclusive tattooist of the St. Louis
Cardinals' mighty 'bullpen'. Whenever the boys of the
'Gas House Gang' are in town to battle the McGraws or
Superbas, they'll drop by to collect some delectable new
'humdingers'. In fact, one of the lads (whom shall remain
anonymous) has inked upon his hurling wing the names
of Herr Ziegfeld's entire chorus line – what a 'lulu'!

In days passed-by, skin illustrations were etched by
hand, usually in a bluish carbon ink. After years of
careful research, I have patented my own unique system
of electric tattooing in four bright colors based on the
principles of electro-magnetic dynamics. Though I must
acknowledge the past contributions of the innovators Sail-
or Sam O'Reilly and Doctor Thomas Alva Edison (himself
an amateur tattooist of some note), the machines I have

developed are more than mere devices — nay, they should be properly classified as works of fine ART! Henry Ford himself, a close personal friend, has told me on several occasions that if he set his top five engineers a'cracking to create a more effective tattoo-applicator, they might toil for a hundred long years and still fail to improve upon my universally recognized and admired design!

There are a few questions regarding skin illustrations that are commonly asked of me. Here, I will address such queries and hopefully provide answers you will find satiating:

1. Is receiving a tattoo a painful procedure?

The short answer — yes. The application of a skin illustration is an excruciating process when applied by the average tattooist. However, I alone have concocted a unique, patented system based upon thoroughly tested scientific principles that has rendered my technique virtually painless. In fact, many of my valued customers have commented that receiving one of my skin illustrations is not only pain-free, but, in fact, downright pleasant. In addition, I offer for sale within my surgery a tonic wrought from the finest Oriental opiates that will not only ease discomfort but provide a pleasant night's dreams.

2. What is the most unusual skin illustration that you have applied to a customer?

This question has always been a bit of a 'corker' for me, as anyone familiar with my repertoire of motifs will tell you I make a habit of specializing in the complex, the outlandish & the exotic. Offhand, I will usually recall the pock-marked child whose father had me provide the spots of a leopard in order to craft an appearance less garish — the lady of the night who requested a placard upon her bosom stating 'IN GOD WE TRUST; ALL OTHERS AIM HERE!' – or even the dashing young Austrian with windswept hair unto whose upper-lip I inlaid a small box-shaped 'Charles Chaplin'.

3. For whom will you not provide skin illustrations? I am a natural-born American, and, as such, I take great pains to insure that the Sacred Liberty our Lord has blessed upon this Great Nation remains virile, strong & intact. Therefore, the list of those to whom I will not provide service is exceedingly short & succinct. Women are welcome. However, children under the age of ten will only be tattooed with a note of permission from a parent or elder sibling. I do not discriminate by race – both tame chinamen and redskins are welcome; I possess rabbinically approved kosher pigments for sheenies; and darkies are accepted after seven o'clock every last Wednesday.

In conclusion, it is my sincere hope that these words will provide a keener insight into the opulence that is skin illustration. Consider yourself a welcome guest to my surgery and do not be rooked by impostors or would-bes!

I remain, forever yours –

Professor Chas. Wagner esq.

208 Bowery

N.Y. City

**DICK STEELE AWAKENED** to gentle prods. The sailor was nowhere to be found. "Up and at 'em, son! If only we COULD sleep all the livelong day!"

There was a grating smarm to the mummy's comportment that a sober Dick Steele would've erased.

"Now then, m'boy, what'll it be? SCHOONER? Saturday, y'know...schooners halfoff! ALL SIZES! Three to twelve bucks — you choose!"

Lids pinched, Dick Steele struggled to stand.

"Lissen pops...had me a doozy with the ol' lady last night. Bitch just...she just don't know howta lissen! All I wanted was a Pepsi, see? And she wouldn't give it to me! Then she works the nerve up to call me limp-dick! I...I reckon shit maybe got a little rough after that. Now I just need me somethin' to smooth things over...somethin' sweet and maybe just a little bit sad. Reckon you could set me up?"

Surveying Dick Steele careful & slow, the mummy chinfiddled then nodded.

"M'boy, if there's one thing I know in life — it's people! People and people's troubles! And you, sir, are a PEOPLE with TROUBLES! C'mon!"

Swiftly ushered to an aged dental-throne, Dick Steele collapsed atop leather sweatmoist.

"Yeah pops, sure...got me some troubles...but so what? I mean, really though —who fuckin' don't?"

Clapping once loudly, the mummy yawped.

"Too right, m'boy! Absolutely, positively too right! But — enough — no more such hooey! Have we convened on this Earth to bicker over Life's indecipherable meaning? Is it not wiser simply to LIVE? And what I am about to provide you, m'boy, is the goshdarndest affirmation of LIFE you'll ever find! So then...what's it gonna be? How shall we erase that long face? There's a MAGIC inside these skin illustrations! Thousands worldwide will testify! My pigments contain jujus fit to shame any aboriginal witchdoctors! In addition — they'll cure asthma, gout, bleakness & rickets! Express thyself, dear sir! In short: THY WISH IS MY MOST HUMBLE COMMAND!"

Sleevefurling, forearm-appraising, Dick Steele brushed gelled crust from coarse curls.

"Aw gee...gotta make things right by this broad...maybe just slap a heart right over here. Make it say Violet real pretty! That oughta do it...think she'll like it..."

Adjusting its visor, the mummy beamed joy — red nose aping a whore's bulb. "Certainly! That's possible! That's my motto here — POSSIBLE! In fact, I've erased IM-possible from the ol' lexicon! Simply no use for it! One magic heart coming right up! Guaranteed luck for life, plus six months barring cremation!"

Upon a straightrazor's sudden approach, Dick Steele reared back to strike. "WHAT'S THE BIG IDEA?"

"M'boy...please remain calm! Simply need to defuzz your arm...a mere technicality! No monkey-biz — I wholly & humbly assure you!"

Dragging its sponge across Dick Steele's limb, the mummy shaved & then greased. A strange brass device had begun to clatter, though no switch had been thrown.

**PAUSING MIDWAY,** the mummy set its odd tool upon a glass counter then lifted a second contraption.

Vermeil goo sputtered from six tiny teeth.

"And what's that for?"

"RED, m'boy! RED! Every good skin illustration has plenty of red! Why, RED is the color of LOVE!"

"Yeah, and Russia and Gilda & blood..."

"Yes! Haha! And blood! That too! "

Standing aloft, device-to-heart, the shirtless mummy boomed sonorous. "I WAS A QUEEN AND YOU TOOK AWAY MY CROWN! A WIFE AND YOU KILLED MY HUSBAND! A MOTHER AND YOU

DEPRIVED ME OF MY CHILDREN! MY BLOOD
ALONE REMAINS — TAKE IT, BUT DO NOT
MAKE ME SUFFER LONG!"

But...wha? Jesus Cripes, a queen?

A sallow left eye twitched queerly once before the
mummy piled Dick Steele stonedead. Shaking free of
the corpse, he hollered — rousing a barber napping
beneath an IL PROGRESSO bulldog.

Scuttling rearwards, handmirroring a grin,
the barber commenced pocketforage.

"Yes, I a'knew this a'day would a'come sometime
soona! God a'bless him...sweet a man as they a'come!"

"But...fella said he was a queen...wouldn'ta figgered..."

Two long shadows slid corpsewise.

Dick Steele turned and then cringed.

Trenchcoated brutes obscured a doorjamb — one
dangling a goresmeared brassiere, the other holsterca-
ressing. Glancing down to his unfinished totem,
Dick Steele's pale lips trembled.

# V - I - O - L - E - N - T

"**IN THE CONCLUDING SEGMENT** of this
evening's SEE IT NOW, I'll be speaking with
Doctor Fredric Wertham, former chief psychiatrist of the Bellevue Hospital's Mental
Hygiene Clinic in New York City and current
chairman of the Lafargue Psychiatric Clinic
in Harlem. Since emigrating from Germany
following World War One, Doctor Wertham has
had a very long, distinguished career here in
America and we're quite pleased to have this
opportunity to speak with him. Welcome, sir."

"Thank you, Mister Murrow.
It is very good to be here."

"Doctor Wertham, correct me if I'm wrong,
but this reporter seems to recall you being
prominent in the news a while back. Perhaps
as far as some twenty years ago. This was
during the infamous 'BROOKLYN VAMPIRE'
trial here in New York City. Is this correct?"

"Yes, Mister Murrow, that IS correct! That
was the FISH trial — a very sad case indeed! I
testified on behalf of the defense that
Albert Fish was insane..."

"That's right. Refresh my memory though.
Were your efforts successful?"

"That all depends on your personal defini-
tion of SUCCESS, Mister Murrow! While the
jury & judge unanimously agreed that Mister
Fish was indeed insane — he was EXECUTED
regardless of this fact!"

"I see. Rarely in life are things ever black &
white, especially concerning issues of morality...and particularly when harm comes to
children...the Vampire Trial being
a prime example of this."

"Rarely BLACK & WHITE — that's quite
CLEVER, Mister Murrow, considering what
I'm here to DISCUSS today!"

"Unintentional...I assure you. Ladies and
gentleman, Doctor Wertham is here to discuss what he sees as a DISTURBING TREND
regarding the influence of four-color comic
books on America's youth. Doctor Wertham

believes that these COMIC BOOKS have been a primary contributing factor to the alarming increase of juvenile delinquency. Doctor Wertham, did I sum that up correctly?"

"Yes — I would say that is fair."

"Doctor Wertham, I've read your recent articles and found some of your arguments quite compelling. Talk to us about these CRIME & HORROR comic books and try to explain some of their negative impacts."

"CERTAINLY! My only question is WHERE to begin, my complaints are so MYRIAD! As you well know, the public has judged television much more harshly than it has comic books. That comes from the fact that adults actually SEE television, whereas, as a rule, they have no idea what comic books their children really read or what is IN them! There are all kinds of atrocities in these 'MAGAZINES'! One may pick up a comic book at random and find several tales in which the stories of murder go from the simple to the gruesome to the WEIRD — all in the same book!"

"I see..."

"One man kills his wife with a poker, another shoots a wolf which is his wife, a third man becomes transformed into a huge crab and eats his wife! An 'AUTOPSY' is performed on a man who is still alive and he screams on the coroner's table! An artist ties the hands of his model to the ceiling, stabs her & uses her blood for paint! A very sexy-looking girl tells

her husband that she is pregnant. He opens
his jacket and the girl looks at him, horrified!
There are gears & pistons! He tells her, 'YOU
COULDN'T BE EXPECTING MY CHILD, NOW
— COULD YOU, MEIN FRÄULEIN? NOT VERY
WELL WHEN YOUR HUSBAND IS A ROBOT!'
You will find this type of 'VARIETY' in the
average crime comic! I must also say that I
do not mean to imply that ALL television is
harmful! There are many EXCELLENT chil-
dren's shows...like MR. I. MAGINATION, UN-
CLE LUMPY, MISTER WIZARD, KUKLA, FRAN
& OLLIE, and PAUL WHITEMAN'S TV CLUB.
And, of course, SEE IT NOW..."

"I thank you for the kind endorsement, sir
— as do our rival networks! But please, go
on...I'd like to hear more about these
crime comic books..."

"Well...in another comic book the criminal
is a police lieutenant. He kills his wife by
deliberately running over her with his car!
At the end, he is undetected & completely
unsuspected and presumably lives happily
ever after! Six pictures on one page show this
policeman-murderer lighting and smoking
a cigar — walking triumphantly with the full
knowledge that crime DOES pay! He goes free
because at the police station an innocent man
is tortured into making a confession! The
child reader is spared NO details! The man is
punched in the stomach, hit in the face, his
arm is twisted behind his back! Mind you...I

am only describing stories that are written,
drawn & printed! I see the results of these
monstrosities in my clinic on an almost-daily
basis — and what happens in real life
is often far WORSE!"

"Describe, if you will, a typical patient."

"I recently had to examine a young man facing jailtime in order to give an expert opinion
about his sanity for the courts. He was in serious trouble, being accused of attempted rape.
He had enticed a girl to walk with him past
a vacant lot & then suddenly pounced upon
her. The girl had stated that there was no
actual rape and that she got away from him
— bruised & with her clothes torn. I told the
young man that I wanted to know more about
his life and he told me his story. Since childhood, he'd had fantasies of tying a girl up, especially tying her hands behind her. It started
when he was about eleven and saw pictures of
that in WONDER WOMAN comic books. From
then on, he looked for comic books where
THAT — the act of BONDAGE — was especially
depicted! For example, those with girls tied in
chairs with their hands fastened behind their
backs. He cut out these comic book pictures
& also he drew them himself. They gave him
sexual fulfillment! He had no intention of
actually RAPING the girl — an act of which he
would have been less ashamed. All he wanted
to do was to BIND her! The struggle to do it
had given him full sexual satisfaction! This is

a typical example of the cases that made me resolve to study the comic book question systematically..."

"I can certainly SEE how that might compel you. Doctor Werthstein, some of your articles have described teenage dope-shooting and the role comic books have played in THIS epidemic as well."

"WerthHAM! And yes, this is true regarding the narcotic usage — a very sad dilemma indeed!"

"Could you please elaborate on this?"

"Well, we have known about childhood drug addiction for some time! It was one of the Lafargue guidance counsellors who brought the first child drug-addict to my official attention. This boy of fourteen had come and asked for help. 'I AM A MAINLINER,' he said. 'I WANT TO GET RID OF THE HABIT. I HAVE BEEN POPPING MYSELF — HITTING THE MAINLINE!' He rolled-up his sleeves and showed me the sores on his arm. He had a needle with a plain eyedropper attached with which he had given himself injections. A regular hypodermic needle was too expensive for him! He had been STEALING to buy the narcotics! When I asked him where he had learned to make such an apparatus. he said, 'FROM THE CRIME & MURDER COMICS. THEY SHOW YOU EVERYTHING!'"

"I see, that is INDEED disturbing. Now, Doctor Wertham...is it just the crime comic books

and the horror comic books, or do you take
umbrage with other forms and varieties?"

"Certainly, yes!"

"Such as?"

"Jungle comics are, to me, also crime
comics of a SPECIAL branch!"

"No pun intended, I assume."

"Certainly not! Jungle comics specialize in
TORTURE, BLOODSHED & LUST in an exotic
setting! Daggers, claws, guns, wild animals,
overdeveloped girls in brassieres & as little
else as possible; dark 'NATIVES', fires, stakes,
posts, chains, ropes! Big-chested and heav-
ily muscled Nordic he-men DOMINATE the
stage! These jungle comic books contain such
details as one girl squirting fiery 'RADIUM
DUST' on the protruding breasts of another;
white men battering well-meaning, simple
natives; close-up views of BREASTS being
BRANDED; a girl about to be BLINDED! All
this type of stuff can be found in SHEENA,
NYOKA, and what-have-you! And while the
white people in jungle books are blonde, athletic & shapely — the idea conveyed about the
natives is that there are only fleeting transi-
tions between apes & Negroes! I have repeatedly found in my studies that this character-
ization of colored peoples as SUBHUMAN,
in conjunction with depictions of forceful
heroes as blond Nordic supermen, has made
a deep, and I believe, LASTING impression
upon young children! And amidst all the

violence between slaves, apes & humans in
these books are big pictures of LUSH GIRLS...
as nude as the US Post Office permits! Even
on an ADULT, the impression of sex plus violence is quite definite in jungle comics!"

"Interesting..."

"Yes — that is ONE way of putting it!"

"And your thoughts on the romance comics
that seemingly every teenage girl
in America devours?"

"Ach...the 'HEADLIGHT' comics..."

"Headlight?"

"Amongst boys, 'headlights' refers to the
BREASTS! There was a boy from a well-to-do
family who was referred to me for psycho-
therapy after he had become very inattentive
in his studies. During treatment, he told me
once that he and two other boys, ages fifteen & sixteen, used to go to a candystore in
the neighborhood where they ate ice cream
cones, bought comic books, and talked 'BIG'
like boys will do. One evening, in one boy's
parents' car, they drove from the suburbs,
where they lived, to Times Square. There, they
picked up a young prostitute and took her
to the home of one of the other boys whose
parents were away in Europe. Two of them
had intercourse with the prostitute and performed various sexual experiments — the
girl being very co-operative. They paid her
five dollars each. After that, all three went
out with her in the car to drive her back to

Manhattan as they had promised. On the way, they had a bright idea. They stopped the car, pounced upon the girl, and, while one held her forcibly around the neck, the others BEAT HER unmercifully about the face & body! They went through her handbag and took out all her money. One boy, hitting her in the face, said to her, 'YOU ARE TOO DARNED INDE-PENDENT!' The girl did not fight back! She just sat there and cried and said it was not fair. After all, she had been so nice to them. Then, they left her at a subway station with just enough money to pay her fare. This is what America's children learn
in ROMANCE comic-books!"

"I see. Rather salty stuff, even for ten thirty."

"I apologize, Mister Murrow — I am simply here to tell the TRUTH!"

"But, Doctor Wertham, what about 'CLAS-SIC' comics? You know...the variety that re-tell great stories & literature of the past? Do these have no educational merit as well? Do these too, in your opinion, ALSO inspire crime & degeneracy? My own ten year-old son — an honor student — has seemed to derive a great deal of both pleasure & knowl-edge from this variety of comic book."

"I'm sorry to tell you that I do not approve of these either! There is a great misconception amongst the general population regarding 'CLASSIC' comic books! Comic books adapted from classical literature are reportedly used in twenty five thousand schools in the United States! If this is true, then I have not yet heard a more serious INDICTMENT of the low quality of American education! These 'CLASSIC' comics utterly emasculate the books they claim to adapt! They condense them and leave out EVERYTHING that makes the books great! Additionally, they are just as badly-printed & inartistically-drawn as any other comic books! They do NOT reveal to children the world of good literature — which has at all times been the mainstay of liberal & humanistic education! Quite the CONTRARY...they CONCEAL it! After being processed in this way, no classic comic, no matter who wrote it, is in ANY way distinguishable from the floppity-rabbit and crime comics it is supposed to replace!"

"But...to be fair...Doctor Wertham, I've looked at these 'CLASSIC COMICS' myself and have found some to be marvelous adaptations of their source material. I wouldn't let my own son read them otherwise..."

"Ah...perhaps so! But supposing your son gets used to eating sandwiches made with very strong seasonings — with onions and peppers and highly-spiced mustard — he will soon lose his taste for simple bread & butter, and for FINER foods as well! The same is true of reading strong comic books!"

"I'll bear that in mind at the drugstore. Doctor Wertham, in your articles you've also expressed problems with the so-called 'SU-PERHERO' genre. You've taken particular pains to stress your issues with BATMAN, SUPERMAN & WONDER WOMAN. Could you elaborate on this for us please?"

"Certainly. I have naturally emphasized these PARTICULAR characters as they appear to be the most widely-read of the 'SUPER-HEROES'! My attention to this dilemma was piqued several years ago when a fellow psychiatrist pointed out that the BATMAN stories are PSYCHOLOGICALLY HOMOSEXUAL! Our research at the Clinic confirms this entirely! Only someone ignorant of the fundamentals of psychiatry & of the psychopathology of sex can fail to realize the subtle atmosphere of homoeroticism which pervades the adventures of the mature BATMAN & his young friend ROBIN! Just as ordinary crime comic books contribute to the fixation of violent and hostile patterns by suggesting definite forms for their expression — so the BATMAN stories help to fixate homoerotic tendencies by suggesting the form of a Ganymede/ Zeus love-relationship!"

"Doctor Wertham, I'm afraid you have me at a disadvantage. It's been many years since my college-days. 'Ganymede' refers to WHOM exactly?"

"He was a mortal that the Greek god Zeus kidnapped, seduced & enslaved as his homosexual lover!"

"I see. Thank you for that clarification."

"As I was saying, Batman & Robin — 'THE DYNAMIC DUO' — go into action in their special uniforms! They constantly rescue each other from violent attacks by an unending number of enemies! The feeling is conveyed that we men must STICK TOGETHER because there are so many villainous creatures who have to be exterminated! They lurk not only under every bed, but also behind every star in the sky! EVERY DAY, Batman & his young boyfriend are captured, threatened with every imaginable weapon, almost crushed to death or annihilated! Sometimes Batman ends up in bed injured and young Robin is shown sitting next to him...FAWNING! At home, they lead an IDYLLIC life, where they are BRUCE WAYNE & DICK GRAYSON! Bruce Wayne is described as a socialite and the OFFICIAL relationship is that Dick is Bruce's ward! They live in sumptuous quarters with beautiful flowers in large vases & they have an effete butler named ALFRED! Batman is sometimes even shown in a DRESSING GOWN! As they sit by the fireplace, the young boy Dick worries about his partner! 'SOMETHING'S WRONG WITH BRUCE. HE HASN'T BEEN HIMSELF THESE PAST FEW DAYS!' It's like the WISH-DREAM of two homosexuals living together! Sometimes they are shown on a couch — Bruce reclining and Dick sitting next to him — jacket off, collar open, and his

hand on his friend's arm...like
the GIRLS in other stories!"

"An interesting take."

"It is the OBVIOUS take! Robin is a handsome, ephebic boy, usually shown in his uniform with bare legs! He is buoyant with energy & devoted to nothing on Earth as much
as to Bruce Wayne! He often stands with his
legs spread — the GENITAL-REGION dis-
creetly evident! And, in these stories, there
are practically NO decent, attractive, or successful women! A typical female character is
THE CATWOMAN, who is vicious and uses a
WHIP! The atmosphere is HOMOSEXUAL &
ANTI-FEMININE! If the girl is good-looking —
she is undoubtedly the villainess; if she is after Bruce Wayne — she will have NO CHANCE
against Dick! For instance, Bruce & Dick go
out one evening in dinner clothes, dressed
exactly alike. The attractive girl makes forward gestures toward Bruce while in succes-
sive pictures young Dick looks on, smiling
mockingly — certain of Bruce's
devotion to him!"

"I wonder how ROBERT KANE — the cartoonist who created & draws Batman —
would respond to such analysis..."

"Mister Murrow, I should be MORE than
pleased to speak with Mister Kane anytime,
anywhere! Please note that I am not accusing
him of DELIBERATELY creating & dissemi-
nating homosexual propaganda — sometimes

these things occur UNCONSCIOUSLY! But the HARD FACTS remain TRUE! I have personally examined many overt homosexuals being treated at our Readjustment Center to find out what they thought about the influence of these BATMAN stories on children! A NUMBER of them knew these stories very well and spoke of them as their favorite reading material! One young homosexual brought me a copy of DETECTIVE COMICS featuring a Batman story! He pointed out a picture of 'THE HOME OF BRUCE AND DICK' — a house beautifully-landscaped, warmly-lighted & showing the devoted pair side-by-side looking out a picture window! He told me that when he was just EIGHT, he'd realized from fantasies about comic book pictures that he was AROUSED by MEN! He said, 'AT THE AGE OF TEN OR ELEVEN, I FOUND MY LIKING, MY SEXUAL DESIRES, IN COMIC BOOKS. I IMAGINED MYSELF IN THE POSITION OF ROBIN. I WANTED TO HAVE RELATIONS WITH BATMAN! THEY SEEM TO BE SO CLOSE TO EACH OTHER. I REMEMBER THE FIRST TIME I CAME ACROSS THE PAGE MENTIONING THEIR SECRET BATCAVE. THE THOUGHT OF BATMAN AND ROBIN LIVING TOGETHER AND POSSIBLY HAVING SEX-RELATIONS CAME TO MY MIND!'"

"Ladies and gentleman, if you're just tuning in, my guest is Doctor Fredric Wertham of Harlem's Lafargue Clinic. He's speaking

with us about subversive elements found in
'superhero' comic book magazines amongst
other varieties of comic books..."

"Thank you, sir. Now, the LESBIAN counter-
part of BATMAN may be found in the stories
of WONDER WOMAN! The homosexual con-
notation of the Wonder Woman type of story
is PSYCHOLOGICALLY UNMISTAKABLE! For
BOYS, Wonder Woman is a frightening image!
For GIRLS, she is a MORBID IDEAL! Where
Batman is anti-FEMININE, the attractive
Wonder Woman & her counterparts are definitely anti-MASCULINE! Wonder Woman has
her OWN female following! They are all con-
tinuously being threatened, captured, almost
killed! There is a great deal of mutual rescu-
ing — the same type of rescue fantasies as in
Batman! Her followers are called the 'HOLLI-
DAY GIRLS'! Wonder Woman often just refers
to them as 'MY GALS'! Their attitude about
DEATH & MURDER is a mixture of the cal-
lousness of crime comics with the COYNESS
of sweet little girls! In a typical story, Wonder
Woman is involved in adventures with another girl — a princess who talks repeatedly
about 'THOSE WICKED MEN!'"

"If I'm not mistaken, this character also car-
ries a lasso with some form of
magic properties?"

"Certainly, yes — each and every Wonder
Woman story features AT LEAST one instance
of this golden rope being utilized to enact

some kind of overtly-sexual BONDAGE!"

"Doctor Wertham, is it true that the Wonder Woman character was itself created by a fellow psychiatrist?"

"No — the late Doctor Marston was a psychologist, NOT a psychiatrist! Much of his life's work has since been discredited as BUNK!"

"I'm told that he was also one of the inventors of the polygraph, which, I believe, is still in regular use by many branches of our military, intelligence agencies & police forces."

"That MAY be so...of this, I am uncertain."

"I'm afraid we're running short on time, but, at the risk of a lawsuit from ABC — let's wrap this up with your thoughts on Superman."

"Certainly! The SUPERMAN comic books present our world in a kind of FASCISTIC setting of VIOLENCE & HATE & DESTRUCTION! Not a very SOUND diet for children, do you think? Actually, Superman, with the big S on his uniform, which I suppose we should be THANKFUL is not an SS, needs an endless stream of ever-new Submen, criminals & 'FOREIGN-LOOKING' people — not only to JUSTIFY his existence, but even to make it POSSIBLE! This engenders in children either one or the other of two attitudes: either they fancy themselves as SUPERMEN, with the attendant prejudices against the Submen, or it makes them submissive & receptive to the blandishments of strong men who will solve all their social problems for them by FORCE!

Additionally, Superman not only defies the laws of GRAVITY, which his great strength makes conceivable, he gives children a COMPLETELY WRONG idea of other basic physical laws! Not even SUPERMAN, for example, should be able to lift up a building while not standing on the ground — or to stop an airplane in mid-air while still flying himself! On even the most BASIC scientific level, this is UNMITIGATED POPPYCOCK!"

"Doctor Wertham, as educational as your visit has been, I'm afraid we've now run out of time. Would you care to directly address the millions of American parents watching this program before signing-off?"

"Why, yes — yes, I would! And I thank you, Mister Murrow, for the opportunity to be heard."

"It's been my pleasure. Just look into that camera. Yes — that's the one. And now... you may begin..."

"Parents of America, set your children FREE! Give them a CHANCE! Let them develop according to their FULL POTENTIALS! DON'T expose them to your ugly passions when they have hardly yet learned to read! DON'T teach them all the violence, the shrewdness, the hardness of your own lives! DON'T spoil the spontaneity of their dreams! DON'T lead them halfway to delinquency and, when they get there, clap them into your reformatories! DON'T stimulate their minds with sex & perversity and label the children 'ABNORMAL' when they react to such stimuli! DON'T continue to desecrate death, graves & coffins with horror stories and degrade sex with the sordid rituals of hitting, hanging & torturing! DON'T sow in their young minds the sadistic details of destruction! These children are our FUTURE & we must PROTECT them accordingly!"

"Doctor Wertham — I thank you, sir. Ladies & gentleman, what you've heard tonight are one learned man's opinions. It is important not to confuse these OPINIONS with FACTS! With all due respect to the doctor, and despite cries to the contrary that certain others will preach or project — the field of psychiatry is undeniably still one in its infancy and we must temper our own personal conclusions with this awareness. We should not be driven by fear into an age of paranoia. We are not descended from fearful men; nor from men who feared to allow their own children the right to form opinions and ideas for themselves. Guidance of our youth is undeniably essential, but of equal value is the virtue of strong, individual character & opinion. Like Doctor Wertham, I TOO believe the children are our future — teach them well and let them lead the way. Goodnight & goodluck."

**SCOURING THIRD AVE** for a vacant phonebooth, Jack Coal nearly capsized with hunger. Despite absorbing three Denvers & a bowl of French Onion — not to mention Bert Meskin's sliced liver — he remained utterly famished.

Atop a sidewalk windy & mobbed, a leering brunette pushed twinstrollers...its passengers sporting blue middies...just like Mister Salty.

Procuring two pretzels from a weeniecart, Jack Coal gnawed pastries in tandem.

**WHEN AN EMPTY BOOTH SURFACED** beneath Thirty Eighth, he spat atop a receiver and hankied. Dot had once contracted syphilis from a payphone — the pursuant cure had been costly.

"Yeah?"

"Yes, hello...that you, Zach?"

"Yeah?"

"Oh great. Hello there — it's Jack!"

"Yeah? Jack who? Know a lotta Jacks!"

"Jack...Jack Coal..."

"Ah! Jackie-boy...THE DEVIANT!"

"Ha! Yes, that's me — at your service!"

"How's tricks? WhaddyaknowWhaddyasay?"

"Well, Zach, Pretty good considering...but things... things have been better. Ups, downs. You know."

"Yeah...yes...sure do."

"But let me be frank — "

"'Preciate that, Jack! Busy man these days! Pencillin' eight books a month now!"

Testes tightened & throbbed.

"Zach...Will...Will Meiser is canceling Elastic Man."

"Aw geez, Jack — sorry t'hear that! Know ya

crammed lotta work n'heart inta that book!
Really admired it too..."

"You...you did?"

"Ya kiddin', man? We ALL did! Me, Joe, Kida,
Burgos! Every MONTH we'd scour yer crap!
Lotta talent there, Jackie!"

"Why...I had no idea! Sincerely flattered! Wouldn't've
envisioned you fellows caring at all! But I appreciate it!
Deeply...sincerely..."

"Yeah, well...I meant it! Talented guy, Jack!
And I'm real sorry 'bout Elastic Man too, see?
Real tough break! But ya hadda REAL GOOD
run on it! N'look at the bright side — ain't a
closed door, it's a new opportunity!"

"Yes, well, actually — speaking of new opportunities
— that's why I'm calling..."

"Hmph. Oh yeah? Go on...lissenin'..."

"Okay. Well, Zach...I'm thinking that I'd like to bring
Elastic Man into the Hyman & Kirby fold!"

A prolonged silence elapsed.

"Um...Zach? You still there?"

"Yeah...here...but what zactly didja mean?"

"Well, I meant EXACTLY just what I said — I'd like
to come work for you fellows and bring Elastic Man
along with me! After all...he is rather flexible!"

"Hah! Jackie-boy — always good for the rich
ones! But...I...I don't really getcha! I mean,
how's that even POSSIBLE? Far as I know,
Book's Meiser-property...ain't it?"

"Well, yes — technically. But I'm trying to work
out some kind of...arrangement..."

"Jack, now...listen...an' don't worry, I'm gonna keep this just between us...but just shoot it straight, 'kay? You even TALKED to Will about this geschäft yet?"

"Well, nope...not YET exactly...but, as you know, he & I have worked together for many years and share quite a good rapport, so I really don't foresee — "

"Don't do it, my friend! Don't even bother..."

"I'm sorry?"

"Said — just don't even fuckin' bother..."

"Well...but why the heck not, Zach? Kinda sending mixed signals here!"

"Jack, don't really glim lotta comics outside yer own, huh? Not really much the fan?"

"Well, more of a newspaper-reader to be honest. And of course I enjoy the classics. But yes, I like comics! Sure! COURSE I do...why, I think they're just swell!"

"An' yet y'ain't noticed Joe and I ain't shat-out a new superhero book in six years?"

"I'm sorry?"

"Just what I said, Jackie! No Blammo, no nothin'! All them types went belly-up two years postwar! Mostly just crime, shtuppies & scary crap for us now..."

"Oh. I see. Well, obviously, I'm aware the industry has shifted a BIT — but certainly trends tend to swing and the oth — "

"Tried bringin' back a pajamaboy year or two ago! Nothin' doin'! Didn't sell shit! Didn't even cover the cost a'the paper!"

" — and I think in time that Elastic Man will — "

"Lissen...Jack...yer a good fella an' I like ya, see? Really do! Honest! An' I'm gonna tell

y'somethin' personal...I don't LIKE Willie
Meiser! Not very much at all. I mean, certain-
ly respect him as an artist, but he pulled some
real crud moves on me back in the service an'
I think he's a firstrate prick! Believe you me —
fuckin' LOVE to get one over on him, see? But
I know that he thinks the world a'YOU, Jackie!
Not a doubt in my mind that he's kept Elastic
Man goin' this long purely outta REGARD!
Hyman keeps tracka all the sales-figgers.
EVERYBODY'S! That's how WE figger on what
to do next! He mentions shit sometimes. Yer
book was fuckin' GREAT, Jackie — but it ain't
turned a flat dime now in years..."
  "Oh. I...I see..."
  "Nothin' else I can help y'with, Jack?"
  **Rapping a cracked verso, waving a rankled tabloid, a
wan blur hopped up & down.**
  "Oh...not really...er...Bert Meskin says 'Hi'."
  "Bert? Bert who?"
  **"Meskin...inker...little guy...bowties..."**
  "Bert Meskin? Jesus Christ, man! Okeh,
brother...good talkin' to ya! Just take care
a'yerself, see? And thanks again for callin'!"
  **A click. A dead line. The phone booth felt like a dirty
glass coffin. Even postexit, Jack Coal felt the presence
of Death. "That was odd, Bert...you & Zach Kirby
have some kind of fallout?"**
  "J-J-J-Jack! Jack! L-l-l-l-l-look!"

EDITOR OF
'CRIMINALS NEVER WIN'
COMIC MAGAZINE SLAYS
DIVORCEE AFTER
11-DAY TRYST
IN GRAMERCY PARK HOTEL

Beneath the headline flapped a cuffed man — cheeks
runny with tears. "Holy smoke, Bert! That's Dick
Steele they're talkin' 'bout here! Good ol' sweet Dick!"

"I kn-kn-kn-kn-kn-kn-know! He b-b-b-b-b-beat her
t-t-to d-d-d-d-death w-w-w-w-with an i-i-iron!"

Jack Coal processed the thought for a moment.

"Reckon he needed to set something straight."

**LESTER BROUGHT HOME** more & more comics
— sometimes ten or fifteen per day. A pile three feet
in height soon loomed by his cot. Queries after the
source of such bounties always triggered six words.

"FAT WHITE MAN IN THE PARK!"

This didn't sit right with Cornell.

He'd been around long enough to know benchwarm-
ers didn't dole funds out of connate goodness. He'd
also learned to divine even the subtlest lavendries —
his livelihood dependent upon such savvy.

His little brother displayed no such tells.

Must be spinning yarns...

"LeeLee, darling, I'm really not cross — really, I'm
not — but I WILL be if you do not begin leveling!
Admit it...been STEALING again, haven'tcha?"

Staring down to shellacked planks, a mien quaking
hung blank. "Ain't been! Ain't done stoled nothin'..."

A long pointer hooked a round chin. Eyes shifted to
a tacked 8"x10" from ROGUES OF SHERWOOD
FOREST. Lester had once been proud that his brother knew John Derek. Now, it meant nothing at all.

"LESTER PHINEAS JACKSON...you DO recall
what that truant-officer said, do you not?"

"But done TOL' ya 'ready — ain't stealed nothin'! Fat
white man GIMME that money! Why can'tcha just

BELIEVE it? You's my brotha, ain'tcha?"

"And why would this stranger...who doesn't know you from Adam...GIFT all of this hardearned cash?"

"Dunno! 'Cause he like me? 'Cause he rich mebbe?"

Releasing his catch, the scholar browfurrowed.

"Okay, little brother. Then I'd like to meet this mysteryman myself. In fact, bring me to him right now."

**BEYOND A BENCH BARREN,** Lester fingered torn rats — but Cornell would hear nothing of it.

"Whole damn city is FULL of those things!"

Back home, Keds butchered floormouldings while a coat was hangered near steam.

"Suppose you know what this means...hmmn?"

Nodding, Lester shed bottoms as Cornell stoolperched. Bending caselike across a thin lap, bracing glutes, he glared rear. "Whup me, Corny, but DON'T mean I lyin'! When I get big, GON' KILL YA!"

A flinching palm fell feathersoft.

"Okay, LeeLee...going to grant the benefit of doubt this time, because I love you & everybody deserves a second chance. We'll go back to that park tomorrow. I sincerely hope this strange white man will be present."

Rising, Lester hissed whilst troublesome flybrass was attended. "Well, don't love you none! UhUh! Not at all! I HATE ya'll! Hate ya! Hate Ma! Hate Pa! Hate that stupid fat man! Hate this whole dang city! Don't care none if it burn like Rome or Chicago!"

"LeeLee, I understand you're upset. Is there anything or anybody that you DON'T hate right now?"

Mulling the thought, Lester rubbed lids dry.

"Don't hate Bobby the chink! Least he be my friend!"

Rifling through comics, hands coiled a sheaf.

"And where do you think you're going with those?"
"Leave me be, Corny! Just up to the roof —
need me some privatetime now!"

**LATCHING THE DOOR,** Cornell sighed as orbs
drifted toward an ironing-board. Atop floral cotton
THE DEADLY PERCHERON lurked — a book
long-shelved & neglected. Brushing crayons aside, he
spied an endpage: to korny i love u from lester.

**"IF YOU'LL PARDON MY SAYING**...I AM a tad
disappointed!"
"And why's that, sir?"
"No 'coonskin' cap!"
Estes Kefauver chuckled.
"Only sport it when TIME takes my picture!"
The senator had insisted upon occupying Dr. Wer-
tham's own chair; behind Dr. Wertham's own desk;
within Dr. Wertham's own office.
Symptomatic of possible secondary mania.
"So, Doc...some kinda show you put on CBS other
night! SOME KINDA SHOW! Never thunk anyone
coulda got that Murrow fellow so durn plumbfidgety
— but golddurn my hide if you didn't!"
"Perhaps so, but this was not my intention!
I simply iterated cold truths!"
"And this man in the papers...this DICK STEELE
hombre...y'say he works in funnybooks too?"
"Yes, Mister Senator — though I'd venture to add his
brand of 'literature' is not-so-funny indeed!"
Foraging a calfskin attaché, the old man
dropped pulp to a blotter.
"And these funnybooks here...I presume
are fruits of the aforementioned?"

"You would be correct, sir! These are the six most recent issues of his primary venture, CRIMINALS NEVER WIN — a murder comic book of the most sordid variety!"

Surveying the pile, the senator scowled towards a cover lurid & orange. Above a flaming gas-range, a pinstriped ethnic wrangled blonde flesh, digits knuckledeep as he vised.

'YOU COOKED MY GOOSE WITH THEM BULLS, BABY! NOW I'M GONNA COOK YOUR FAT FACE!'

"I'll admit, Doc, that this is rather...disturbing material...and that the circumstances behind its creator make it all the more discomforting...but c'mon now, sir...this here's America not Germany! We don't take kindly to censorship here! Surely this kinda stuff's at least INTENDED for the adult-market!"

"Aha! One would THINK so, yes? Or at least HOPE! The reality is that CRIMINALS NEVER WIN, with a circulation of roughly THREE MILLION — more than that of even the great SUPERMAN — is the most widely-read comic magazine in North America today by children! The bulk of its readership are WELL BENEATH TWELVE YEARS-OLD!"

Desnouting hornrims, the senator pinched his bridge as the old man watched with rapt interest. Early Parkinson's? Huntington's perhaps?

"However, Herr Senator, the CONTENT of the stories are not the only problem! The ADVERTISE-MENTS are just as harmful! Perhaps even more so! Please, I beseech you, looklook..."

Extracting a midpile specimen, Estes Kefauver

**chuckled as tips grew smudged & chromatic.**

Tired of all that extra padding? No date to the dance? Try Reduct-O — the miraculous new technique from Europe that will help you trim that flab away like a hot knife through butter! Proven scientific technique guarantees a loss of ten pounds in first week! No pills! No exercise! No annoying dieting! Start reducing in comfort today!

(ONLY $5.95 — limited time!)

A skinny scarecrow figure is neither fashionable nor glamorous! Skinny Girls are NOT Glamor Girls! Ashamed of your skinny, scrawny figure? Don't let them snicker, do something about it! Estro-Fem can help you to add pounds and pounds of firm attractive flesh to your figure! Checked by our medical director — a well-known New York practicing physician. Remember, the girls with the luscious seductive curves get the dates!

($2.00)

**Pausing, chuckling again, the senator tapped Mamie Van Doren. "Apparent contradictions at play!"**

I BROKE HIS HAND LIKE A MATCHSTICK! It was easy! He was helpless! He howled with pain! Method of Offensive Defense based on natural, instinctive impulse-action! Smashing, crashing, bone-shattering, nerve-paralyzing method!

70 BONE-BREAKING SECRETS!

($1.00 — formerly sold at $5.00!)

**"Nothing wrong with this either, Doc — far as I see!**

Judo's a healthy, normal pastime!"

"But please...read on! Why not try page fifty three?"

FROM A SKINNY WEAKLING
TO A MIGHTY MAN!

I gained 53 lbs of MIGHTY MUSCLE! 6 and a half inches on my CHEST! 3 inches on each ARM! You can do it in 10 minutes a day! Make YOUR Body Bring You FAME instead of SHAME! Are You Skinny? Weak? Flabby? I know what it means to have the kind of body that people pity! I don't care how old or young you are or how ashamed of your present physical condition! I can shoot new strength into your old backbone, help you cram your body so full of pep, vigor & vitality that you won't feel there's even standing room left for weakness!

Estes Kefauver again rubbed his nose. There was no headache, he simply pined a stiff drink. "But Doc... heck's wrong with this one? You tellin' me CHARLES ATLAS is harmful to America's youth?"

"This is correct!"

"And just how's that? I've met the man myself and I like him! Fella's built an empire from nothin' — just teachin' people to be healthy & strong!"

"Sir, advertisements for boys cover different areas but appeal to the same kind of susceptibility to juvenile hypochondriasis as those for girls! The concern of boys with growth & bodybuilding has been exploited for years now! They make the smaller boys feel SHAME about their bodies! And often in these advertisements, with photographs of supermuscular he-men, they take great pains to portray oversized genitals — just like some of the comic book heroes! Look very closely, if you will, at that photo of Herr Atlas...boys with latent & not-so-latent homosexual tendencies COLLECT these pictures! They clip them! Use them for sexual stimulation! One of my patients started to cull these photos at the age of only eleven! By twelve, he had prostituted himself to lechers! Does this sound HEALTHY & STRONG to you?"

**MILLARD GAINES STUDIED** chow mein as candleflicks danced across glaze.

"Eat! Gonna get cold! It's no fuckin' good all cold!"

Glancing north, beyond Al Feldberg, Gaines drank in soft lanternglows. Lights throbbed in harmony with each beat of his heart. The husky man was happy. So very happy, he entertained thoughts of traversing the table to plant a kiss big, wet & sloppy.

"No thanks, ain't my type...too Rubenesque!"

"Wow, you some kinda mindreader now? How'd the fuck y'know what I was thinkin'?"

"Because ya DIDN'T think it, asswipe — you said it!"

Smirking, draining plum wine, the husky man swiveled stretched limbs. "Bottle! FRESH one this time!"

Al Feldberg's limp pompadour wagged.

"Like them pills, eh? Glad they're givin' ya zip, but better chow down — gonna need ya some fuel..."

Slaps giddy thwacking specked cloth rattled dried noodles & salt. "But I'm just too damned HAPPY to eat! Feelin' like Superman these days!"

Eyes fuzzed re-examined chow mein.

"Is kinda pretty though..."

"Goddamned right 'tis — Ruby's don't fuck around!

Gimme that shit if ya ain't gonna touch it!"

Seizing the dish, Al Feldberg rasped betwixt chomps. "Anyhow, Mill...got us a problem..."

"Problem! Always a problem!" The husky man shrugged. "So handle it! That's what I pay y'for, right?"

The editor nodded. "Yeah, Mill. Yeah...guess so..."

"So what's it this time? Graham sozzled again? Should we send him to the cure? Would his pride allow that? Is he too uppity to accept our help? Do Catholics even TAKE the cure? Does it go against scripture? There's so many things that I just don't know! I feel so lost! So very, very lost! You ever feel lost, Al? Eh, probably not! Too strong...too stoic..."

A belch fled a maw greaseslick.

"Nah, ain't that. I mean...yeah, guy's a certified wreck — but, then again, when ain't he? Long as he hits deadline, he can chug BATTERY-ACID all I fuckin' care! Livers ain't nunna my beeswax or yours! But this WERTHAM cat...oh baby! HIM...he fuckin' is!"

"Worse trim? What's that?"

"Kraut shrink — runs a clinic up in Browntown! Fucker's gonna make us kaput soon 'less we do somethin' about it! And I DO mean soon!"

Reclaiming his entrée, the husky man shoveled.

"Whatcha mean though? What for would a shrink wanna hurt US? I love shrinks! Pretty sure I bought mine a bungalow in Palm Springs last year!"

"Because...this particular shrink DON'T like us none and he's got him a big fuckin' mouth! Cat's been clangin' lids 'bout the evil'a funny-books an' teevee! Says we're turnin' kids delinquent & queer! Says Batman's been usin' Robin's schwanz to pogo! TENDER

KISSES made some prepschoolers roll a hooker and God KNOWS what fuckin' else! Shoulda heard this nut on Murrow...unfuckin'believable! Don'tcha watch Murrow no more? You usta love him!"

Millard Gaines cleansed lenses filmy with schmaltz.

"Murrow y'say? Hence the bump in hatemail?"

"Yeah...might have somethin' to do with it..."

"But...c'mon! We publish QUALITY material! For Chrissake...half our readership is ADULTS!"

"Think I don't know — don't preach at the choir! That AIN'T the half he's yappin' bout!"

"Well...okay, but what can WE do? Put a hit out? C'mon, Al...you & me are no sorta heavies..."

Leaning forwards, Al Feldberg whisped. "Lissen, been talk 'bout some kinda Senate-posse convenin'. That happens — we're screwed! All we built...straight down the toilet! Just one big fuckload'a nothin'!"

"But Al, nothing goes STRAIGHT down the toilet... it winds and it shimmies & curves!"

"This AIN'T fuckin' funny, man! This is serious... serious as fuckin' cancer! Cancer'a the fuckin' DICK!"

"Okay...relax! I get it! But where's all this information comin' from? Far as I know, it's just a buncha rumors!"

"Ain't rumors, Mill! My Cousin Solly works in Gulotta's office! He HEARS things! Sees 'em sometimes too."

"Then how's 'bout we get Cousin Solly on this?"

"How, schmuck! He's just a punk clerk!"

"Okay...but Gulotta...he's not in Congress? What would HE have to do with all this?"

"Aw, them bigwigs is all chummy with the other. Gaggle of 'em was up there other day. Sol heard it all..."

Gnaws paused, Millard Gaines cringed.

"Ugh...NO...don't tell me...goldenboy, right? Mob-buster? Peckerwood? Keyflower?"

"KEFAUVER...yeah, he's one'a 'em. And Mill, gets worse...your name was brought up too. More'n once! Much more'n once! That's why Solly called..."

A husky face was thrust into spread palms.

"And you're tellin' me NOW?
Just at the brink of NIRVANA?"

"Yeahyeah...haha...all a big joke! Seriously, Mill — we gotta fuckin' DO somethin'!"

"But Al, tell me...if Frank Costello couldn't stop this guy, the hell WE gonna do?"

A lipglued tentacle swung.

"And that means what? Just roll over and die? Mill, what about me? All'a the boys? Yer RICH, man — ain't GOTTA worry! But I got KIDS! Fact...lotta us do!"

"Okay, Jesus! OKAY! So lay it out...what CAN I do? It's Congress — not Traffic-Court!"

"Could testify! Tell 'em what's what & where t'get off! Can talk pretty good when ya get a mind to..."

"Hmmn..."

Withdrawing brown glass from a coatpocket, the husky man bit a small cork. "Know, Al...had you made that very suggestion a few weeks back, woulda called ya meshugganah! But NOW...now that I'm SUPER-MAN...okay! DEAL, alright? Anything for a pal! My asking-fee: just one minor concession..."

"This again? Jesus...no...can't fuck my wife..."

"Buddy...least let me watch from the closet!"

**ESTES KEFAUVER SMOKED** on the bed and
sneered at the distended package — slowly unfurling
red thread, cursing lobsters & stingers.

BOY — TEN:

Referred to the clinic after shoving a younger child into the East River. Case dismissed
as 'ACCIDENTAL DEATH'. He'd previously
thrown stones at windows & on one occasion
had seriously injured a mentally retarded
adult. Voracious comic book reader. After several months of nonprogress — lobotomized.
Still refuses to give up comics.

BOY — NINE:

Treated at clinic for a behavioral disorder. Daydreams about murder. Explained
he likes CLASSIC COMICS & WOODIE THE
WOODPECKER. Told him I was very much
interested in all varieties of comic books. He
then confided that what he likes most of all is
crime comics. 'I want to be like Machine Gun
Kelly — ice squares & buy flashy neckties.'

BOY — SEVEN:

Suffers from asthma & shyness. Inattentive
in school. Instead of ballplaying, he pores over
comic books. I weaned him away from them
by providing material with which to draw &
paint, but the comic book spirit is still very
evident within his art. Draws Donald the duck
with a gun. Drawings often display duck rob-
bers shooting duck cops. In another, the duck
robber 'plugs' a doctor named 'QUACK'.

BOY. — TWELVE:

Troubled at school. Father unemployed.

'I don't read the comic books — just smoke reefers & browse pictures. I can read, but I don't care to take the time to. Sometimes, when it's a good story, I'll read it; but you'd be surprised how much you can learn just by looking at pictures. If you have a good mind, you can figure things out plenty swell by yourself. Reading is for sissies anyway.'

GIRL — THIRTEEN:

Repeatedly arrested for solicitation.

Tall. Very boyish appearance.

Q: Which comic books do you enjoy reading?

A: Mostly LADY CRIME SPREE & SHEENA.

Q: And which crimes do such ladies commit?

A: Murder. They marry a man for his life insurance & then kill him & then marry another man & then just go on like that until they finally get caught. Or they might be a taxi-dancer & go gaga for the wrong guy.

Q: What's the fun for you in reading that?

A: Learning the goof-ups of others. Picking up ideas. Getting lowdowns on robbery & sex.

Q: Sex?

A: Yes, plenty of sex. They show you exposed women, men beating up girls, breaking their arms. The fellows read that & they want to try it. Wrestle with girls. They tried it with all the girls around my way. Tied them all up. I asked them what made them do that. They all said they saw it in comics. LUSTBAIT, MURDER INC. But they never tied me up. I'm far too tough for any of them.

BOY — TWELVE:

Nineteen arrests. Prepares own meals.

'I read the comic books to learn how you can get money. Read about thirty a week. I read CRIMINALS NEVER WIN, VENGEANCE & AL-CATRAZ MONTHLY. There was this one case — it was in the back of a factory with some fat receipts & money there. Showed how you get in through the backdoor. I just switched things to the skylight & carried it out the same way — only I had to gat two guards to do it. I know other boys who learned how to do such jobs from comics. A few are dead now. Sometimes I see them floating when I drink beer — but I know that ghosts ain't real so I never get yellow.'

BOY — THIRTEEN:

Filipino. Father recently deceased.

'I learned from crime comics that when you want to hit a man, you don't get face-to-face. Just aim for the back of the neck so it snaps. That's how ROBIN does it. He's offed loads of creeps & he's still only in the eighth grade.'

BOY — FOURTEEN:

Mother deserted family; father works nights.

'In Brooklyn poolhalls, they pay us for pro-tection. If the kikes don't pay up, then we knife the felt. Learned that from CRIMINALS NEVER WIN. Book is well worth each dime.'

BOY — SEVEN:

Poor student. Daydreamer.

Diagnosis: schizophrenic-tendencies.

'Sometimes I read a comic book twelve times a day. I look at the pictures a long time. I just imagine they are real. They go around stabbing people. They have eight knives & they rob a liquor-store. They stab a woman with a knife. They stab two women with a knife. One man started drilling folks: five cops, six women & eighteen niggers. Anybody crossed him, he'd just feed them hot lead & laugh.'

BOY — TWELVE:

Father serving life-sentence for rape.

Tests show him reading at kindergarten-level. Reads fourteen to twenty comic books daily. 'Oh yes, I can read words. GUNS, POLICE, DONALD THE DUCK & ROY ROGERS. When I'm on the subway I can read TIMES SQUARE too — on account that's where mama works.'

BOY — TEN:

Family dwells in squalid quarters. Sleeps in a cot with brothers aged six & nine. Considered quite wise in the ways of the street. 'I like ghost stories in murder comics. They teach you how to curse a fellow & swallow his soul. They teach you how to summon the devil when your mother is naked & stewed.'

BOY — ELEVEN:

Usurped money from children in lower grades. Family lives in basement apartment with rat-holes, broken floorboards, flies & leaky pipes overhead; furniture worn past recognition. Father a drunkard; mother

infirmed. Sleeps in a bed with sister aged
fifteen. 'In the best comics they murder people with shivs & they strangle them too. They
stickup banks & they also shoot dope. My
sister looks at murder comics with me every
night. Some men kill girls because the ladies
are rich. Some just because they think she is
pretty. But women enjoy killing men too. They
take men to dancehalls & jook them in the
back. These are just facts of life.'

BOY — NINE:

Well-kempt home, parents employed; avid
comic book fan regardless. 'I like GANG-
BUSTERS, CRIMINALS NEVER WIN, BAT-
MAN, THE APPARITION. They do murders
like shooting. And girls in underwear do
things to the men too; catch bad men & take
them to the law. Bullets bounce right off
PHANTOM LADY's bazooms. I want to BE her.
Squeeze my own headlights at midnight.'

BOY — TEN:

Repeated first grade thrice. Resides with En-
glish-deficient foster parents. Fifth-floor flat
consists of kitchen & bathroom. Family sleeps
in the tub. 'Funnies help me forget all the bad
things. They poison each other. Dynamite
caves. Girls play men for fools & make them
buy mink coats. Not SUPERMAN though. I
don't know if he even likes girls. I think maybe he's afraid he'll kill them if he hugs them
too hard. I wish he would hug LOIS LANE.
She is sneaky & surely deserves it.'

BOY — TWELVE:

Expelled for classroom masturbation.
Ward of Department of Welfare.

'I read all kinds of comics except them lovey kissy jobs. Don't really like them. Only time I read them is when I've seen all the rest of the comics. Don't really like girls. Don't want to kiss them. Fact is, I just want to kill them.'

BOY — EIGHT:

Parents in tuberculosis sanitarium.

'I don't read mystery comics; they make me devil-dream. But I do like the wolfman because he can change. I want to change too.'

BOY — THIRTEEN:

One of seven Negro siblings. They sleep in bunkbeds; four brothers in the upper-berth, three sisters beneath. 'I really admire THE BATMAN. He swings through windows. Girls always be getting hurted & screaming. Murders in Gotham every night. My sisters scream too when we plays THE BATMAN.'

BOY — ELEVEN:

'Now listen to this: if you see a bathroom window lit up, you know someone's at home. If it's still lit the next day, then no one's home. They leave keys in mailboxes or under mats. If you spot a milk-bottle with a note in it, you'll know the lay alright. Another thing, if you can steal a dog, people will pay a lot of bread to get that dog back, even for the older & smellier ones. Smart as I am, I never thought of this. Got it all out of the comics. Neat, right?'

Incidents from ASSOCIATED PRESS:
Three boys aged six-to-eight years hung a
nude girl from a tree, hands tied behind, then
singed her with lighters & matches. Proba-
tion officers investigating determined that
this was indeed a re-enacted comic-book plot.

An adolescent girl tortured a four year-old
boy — destroying an eye, testicle & three
fingers. Reason: 'JUST FELT LIKE IT.' Comic
books & pornographic material were later
found beneath the adolescent's mattress. The
victim is now too disfigured for schooling.

A boy, thirteen, committed the 'lust murder'
of a girl aged six; later asking the arresting
sheriff for comic books, cigarettes & beer.
Etched upon the sheath of his knife was 'KILL
FOR THE LOVE OF KILLING!' — a slogan orig-
inated within a CAPTAIN BLAMMO story.

Four boys (two of fourteen, one fifteen &
one sixteen) beat the proprietor of a candystore with a hammer. While he was lying on
the floor, one drove a knife into his head with
such force that the hilt snapped. The man,
who somehow survived, is now a vegetable.
The attackers will be freed from juvenile de-
tention upon reaching the age of eighteen.

A nine year-old boy killed a five year-old
girl by stabbing her more than two hundred
times. His schoolyard nickname: THE FLASH.

A ten year-old boy who threw a baby into
a river 'TO FEED HUNGRY CATFISH' later claimed to have been inspired by a story

found within an issue of ELASTIC MAN.

A well-to-do plastic surgeon received an extortion note demanding $50,000 & threatening harm to his daughter. Experts deduced the note was the work of an 'adult white male psychopath under severe emotional strain.' The perpetrator was later revealed to be a fourteen year-old Mexican girl with a large romance & vampire comic book collection.

Two twelve year-old girls robbed a taxi-driver while he was stopped for a traffic light. One of them, who claimed to be 'WONDER WOMAN', pressed a knife into his back while the other tied him up & made him 'TELL THE TRUTH'. They kissed the taxi-driver, who is happily-married, then fondled his genitals. Afterwards, they demanded his money & then fled the scene with his keys, leaving the poor man tied with his pants down.

A boy of eleven poured kerosene over a boy of eight & a girl of twelve then burned the children to death. He was later found hanging from a basement rafter — a large pile of DEVIL'S CANDY comic books were discovered within a nearby toychest.

A thirteen-year-old boy slashed an attractive young teacher eight times in the throat, five times in the groin and — once she had collapsed — masturbated over her as she expired. Authorities were bewildered by the behavior of this boy, who came from a good home background. Over three hundred comic books were later discovered in the attic.

IN SUMMATION:

Children are like flowers.

If the soil is good & the weather is not too catastrophic, they will grow up well-enough.

You do not have to threaten them, you do not have to psychoanalyze them & you do not have to punish them any more than wind and storm punish flowers. Bear in mind, however, that flowers do require nurture — poison will only sicken them.

**RE-ENVELOPING THE SHEAF**, rewinding red string, Estes Kefauver blazed a fresh Lucky and rang the hotel's nightporter. "Help you, sir?"

"Hope so. Y'all got Bromo down there? Feel awful..."

"No sir, but we have Alka-Seltzer."

"That'll do. Send a couple packets up to Room 971."

"Of course. Will there be anything else?"

"Matter of fact — yeah. Need me an outside line. Patch me through to Henning's suite at The Carlyle."

A minute elapsed. A clapper trilled.

"Senator Kefauver?"

"Yup."

"Please hold for your call."

One loud click led to another. "This is Henning."

"Tommy? Keef here."

"Christ, boy — half past two! If I'd known it were you, woulda never picked up!"

Estes Kefauver chuckled.

"And who'd ya think it was? Don't tell me your wife!"

"Was hopin' on Cyd Charisse..."

"Ah Tommy...you know I got more curves than that

biddy — they're just all political! But listen, seriously, wanna run something by you."

"What's up?"

"Well, it's this WERTHAM fella...old kraut... had us quite a chat yesterday up in Harlem."

"Good grief — THAT fuckin' quack? Figures that's where he works!"

"Kay...okay now...but just hear me out. I agree, the hombre's a little eccentric..."

"A LITTLE?"

"And I'll concur that his research is a bit shoddy."

"Just a smidge."

"But...and this is a big 'BUT'..."

"Oh brother — "

"...but I really think we oughtta reconsider his potential! Brought up some real interesting points at our pow-wow! REAL interesting! Fr'instance, were y'all aware golddurned SWITCHBLADES are still poppin' up in these danged rags? I mean...STILL?"

"Yeah, Keef. Hardly a scoop..."

"Well...nobody'd hepped ME to it! How 'bout Charles Atlas, Tommy? Y'all ever look close at his johnson?"

**THE FAT MAN'S SMILE** bleared to sludge upon spying Cornell's dire mien. "Come darling! Come-come! Time to go walkies with Daddy!"

The poodle, snout buried eyedeep, paid these commands no heed; a hole harboring rodent-newborns was rife with sweet wafts of placenta.

"Sir, no disrespect — but my brother here claims that you've bestowed upon him a great sum of money. Is there any truth to this? If so...might I inquire why?"

Orbs dogtrained, the fat man's reply warbled oddly.

"Sorry to say I've no idea what you mean —
never seen this child once before in my life!"

Surging, scowling, Lester struggled to shake a tense
vise. "Mista, you's LYIN'! You fuckin' lie!"

As the poodle ignored beckons further, Cornell
dragged his brother aside. Heels dug, the boy held fast
— rage giving way to appeal.

"PLEASE, MISTA...PLEASE DON' LIE! HE
GONNA WHUP ME! SAY IT TRUE NOW OR
HE GONNA WHUP ME BUT GOOD!"

A shrewd yank brought knees to cement.

"Stop, Corny! Shit fuckin' hurts! Goddamn!"

"Lester Phineas Jackson — will you kindly get up
and walk or shall I carry you home like an infant?"

Orbs desperate scanned stalks parched.

"STELLA! STELLA! C'MERE BOY! COME!"

Easing his grip, the scholar turned slowly
as the poodle lawnbounded with glee.

"Okay...well, yes, I did give him some money! Just a
pittance! No funnybiz, I assure you! He's just a sweet,
adorable child, your son — I simply aimed to spread
some good fortune! Here, take this! And this as well!
Take it all! But please, don't attack! My heart can't — "

"Really, sir, put your money away...."

Sliding onto the bench, patting green planks,
Cornell invoked his most inveigling grin.

"Thousand pardons for any confusion, no disrespect
intended. Just looking out for the boy's interests.
This city...you understand..."

Scooting closer, the fat man simpered as the poodle
growled from warm arms. "How 'bout ME, Corny?
Owe me a zillion pardon!"

"Now run along, LeeLee! Just go play with the doggy while your friend & I become better acquainted..."

As Lester trailed Stella back to the rats, a Stearman dragged a banner 'twixt clouds.

## 'DRINK PEPSI-COLA!'

**AS DOT DRIFTED** upon the fawn couch, Jack Coal rose to palm trousers. Padding off in stockingfeet, he left the television charged to mask noises.

This mission demanded discretion.

In the diningroom corner known as his 'den' loomed a drafting-table unclewrought years prior.

**UNZIPPING HIS CASE,** sliding blank bristol, guilt stabbed Jack Coal's nether region. The board had been filched from the shop-closet.

Thoughts harked an Eastern State visitingroom.

'But Tyrone...why? He was our father.'

'As if your knob never got turned!'

**RAZORING THE BOARD** to six thin sections, vowing to repay Will Meiser, Jack Coal taped a leaf to his table, taking care to ensure it sat level. T-square and HB in hand, ruling five roughly-squared panels, waves of relief swished fleet.

A daily strip! All that he'd dreamed as a young boy! What he should've been doing all along!

Pale digits caressed smooth teeth.

Remember that old correspondence-course?

The Landon School of Cartooning?

He'd dropped to knees and pled with hands clasped, but STILL Dad had refused to help pay. Sandwiches moonlight-crafted were sneaked to class, lunchmoney amassing in trickles.

Had that been stealing? Surely hope not. Can one steal righteously to support a just cause? Had Charles Landon himself not commended McManusian shades?

**FACING PANELS BLANK** for an hour's elapse, ceding victory to sore testes — Jack Coal fled, kitchenbound, hellbent for jarred Nescafé.

Stirring creamer, he lifted the paper.

WORLD-TELEGRAM?

Odd...Dot swears by THE NEWS.

Shrugging, he thumbed to the funnies, intrigued by alien curations. The strange section was larger-than-average, plump with both standard & sapling; most of the latter slapdash affairs — sketchy, all nib/no brush. Six columns down, something called 'Peanuts' glorified pathetic whining.

Jack Coal chuckled at its lack of finesse.

Stupid. Won't last the year.

**JACK COAL'S URINE** ricocheted porcelain in deference to Dot's drooly slumber. Rinsing, jowlsplashing, fingers tensed with sudden disgust.

Old! Fat! Spent!

He tugged the mirror aside.

Behind it, atop a shelf neglected, sat Will Meiser's stale benzedrine. The pile was slapped past a tongue.

**PADDING BACK TO THE DEN**, Jack Coal mulled carting Dot to bed — but a couchpillowed smirk instantaneously dashed this notion. Fetching a blanket, draping curves, hems were tucked à la piecrust as burrows evertightened the shroud.

Good ol' Dottie...snug as a thug in a jug!

Massing tools & yarn, refilling a basket beneath
the TV, a kneedlebound mound begged notice.
Is...is that...is that a sock?
A...tiny...wee...SOCK?
Booties-to-brows obscured Steve Allen's blue scowl.
A pulse banged fiercely aloud.
Good God in Heaven! Glances backwards con-
firmed dull glows. No. Now? Can...can this be?
Dot was...glowing!
Really? After all this time?
But she WAS glowing! GLOWING! GLOWING!
Thoughts raced. Never changed a diaper once
in my life! No matter! Don't I learn quick?
Names! NAMES! Middle-names! Schools! Pic-
nics! Slingshots! Baseball! Sheepdogs!
Again he spun rear. Wake her? No sir — bad
form! Needs all the rest she can scrounge!
Giddy socks fled, hope-imbued.
Glows danced for a cathode ray tube.

**BASKING IN DAWN,** hours on, Jack Coal signed a
sixth daily with gusto. Surveying bristol, pride oozed
from each gland. A grin broadened and wrenched.
Been under his nose the whole damn time!
DOTTY & ME!
The heroic travails of two bonded rats fending despair in the city! Familiar equation? Perhaps, but Le
Grande Switcheroo had been pulled — Junior was
the brains behind THIS outfit, advising grown kin like
Buddha! Pathos...Ingenuity...Laughs...surely, THIS was
a winner! This meant money! BUSHMILLER money! New Milford! Packards! A mink! TEN minks!
Some foxes to keep 'em all company!

Grooming for the post-office, Jack Coal winked through soaplather. Ain't slept a lick & not tired one whit! In plain fact, he'd never felt MORE awake! MORE ALIVE! LESS HUNGRY!

**A STEAMY HALO** framed Tatiana as her husband arrived companion in-tow. Though the strange man was long and lean in a broadshouldered, athletic fashion — a red flattop & tattered green plaid conspired to weave dubious airs.

Visibly soused, Wally Good squinted, backslapped the outlier, then flicked a taut palm towards his wife. "TOTS...Arch Andrews! ARCH...this here's Tots! Get used to each other! Now on, you two's gonna be best pals! Arch here's stayin' for grub!"

Curls were daubed. A wry smirk flashed. "Ach, Wally! Kind of you, but a little notice would've been —"

"Lissen Goody...just gonna fetch me a sandwich down The Blarney — don't wanna put youse out."

"Kiddin'? Best stay right the fuck there if'n ya know what's what!"

"Yeah...well...don't wanna intrude or nothin'..."

A yellowed apron untied. "Herr Andrews, you sit down right now & make it snappy — I have a roast in the oven that'll be more than enough! Rembrandt here eats like the little baby sparrow besides!"

Lips acackle pecked a damp cheek.

"The fuck's solids 'gainst whisky?"

**AS THE GOOD'S TEEVEE** summoned naught but snow, the boys launched nickels at passers below. Tatiana dispensed dinerfilched napkins. Food was ladled atop lapbalanced plates. "Sure is swell, Mrs. Good... really damn swell! Ain't had a homecooked broil since

Uncle Sam nicked me!"

A mane highpiled quivered. "It's not enough salt, is it? Ever since the war, I'm still not using much salt!"

"Nah...s'great, Mrs. Good! Really damn swell!"

Slivers flew from cheeks packed.

"Misses my ASS — that's TOTS!"

"Yes, please. Tatiana. Or just Tots."

Cubes sucked from Four Roses crunched.

"Yessir, this li'l gal here's my only souvenir of Deutschland! Couldn'ta picked any better!"

"Thought I detected a slight accent!"

"You make fun! Not nice, Herr Andrews!"

"ME — kid YOU? Never!"

"Yes-yes...in Germany we met. This man in uniform...so handsome!"

"And this was when? Forty-five?"

"Forty-eight. Was with the Paratroops then — spent the war with the Merchant Marine."

"Wise choice...but why re-hitch after the party?"

"Eh, didn't know fuckall t'do with myself! Seen the world — what was there for me back in Minnesota? Pump gas? Sort mail? No thanks!"

"Duluth? Saint Paul?"

"Not even close...that wouldn'ta been so bad. We were way, way up there. Coal country."

"Folks miners?"

"Nah. Pop's a lumberjack — runs a big camp."

A mien knotted and glared.

"Ach...Wally, you said your papa was dead!"

"To me he is." Eyes dodged south. "Anyhow Arch, what was YOUR war like?"

"Rough! Real rough! Marines loved me so goddamned much — wouldn't let me outta San Diego!"

A slab of broil flung at the outlier's brow slapped flush then remained glued. As freckled knuckles peeled the meat free, Tatiana noted an oversized band. Crudely cast, coarsely ridged, its center harbored a skull & crossed bones.

"That ring, Mister Arch...from where did it come?"

"Ah Tots, that's just some dumb jarhead shit! All these harebrains have 'em!"

Sucking a digit, the outlier lobbed; the band table-struck with a crack. "Nah, Goody...nothin' leather-necky. Broke an ankle in an overturned jeep, spent the liberty in TJ. Found it in a pawnshop down there..."

Lifting, Tatiana focused. Yanking her wrist, Wally Good clucked. "Looks like that crap crooks hawk in comics — know what I mean? Johnson-Smith?"

The outlier waved a verdigris smear.

"Bingo! Guaranteed to tint your mitts green!"

As drinks refilled and smokes shook loose, Tatiana continued to stare — drifting further, across an ocean, to a brooding, nearimpalpable leer.

**MOTHER DRAGGED HER ALONG** every mid-day to deliver Father's bagged lunches. Peter was everpresent; toiling away, in a dark corner, visored & blotprotected.

He'd stare back through greenshaded orbs — perpetually hungry, maw slightly upcurled. Following a litany of moist tantrums, Mother kiboshed mandatory escortage.

**SEVERAL MONTHS ON,** Peter appeared at their doorstep, ferrying documents demanding urgent attention.

One week later — he was back.

Quickly sussing the girl as a household knobturner, supper-disruptions persisted. Sometimes, there would be no papers at all — only the thinnest excuses.

Crying jags butting paternal pshaws were adjudicated girlish ardor haywired.

"I cannot blame you, Herr Jäger is a handsome man — but please do not concern me with feminine trifles! Such matters are to be bandied with Shoshana or Mother..."

And so, the intruder continued to stare.

Eventually, Tatiana surrendered.

**ERRORS GRAVE SURFACED** two years further, necessitating a hasty discharge — Father's table declaim of an acrid withdrawal tainting fine gooseliver & onions.

"He knocked the desk over, papers went flying — much like a bomb's detonation! Then he called me a Jewish swine! A bloodsucking vampire! He claimed to have been nothing more than the most devoted employee despite slave-wages forcing him to suffer in squalor! It was unfortunate. Most unfortunate. And so undignified too. It was disheartening to witness such despair in a man I'd almost considered a son. I don't think he truly MEANT those words! He couldn't have! An apology, no doubt, will be forthcoming. I'm certain of Herr Jäger's return..."

Mother allowed Frida to clear each plate before finally responding. "But Hans, do you truly believe Peter embezzled these funds?"

Fingers stroking manicured whiskers coaxed a blunt bulletshape. "Meine liebste, I do not know. I'd certainly LIKE to believe that he didn't. While I'd prefer to think that within each man's breast beats a pure heart — the fact remains that I am running a business. Whether this money was pilfered or lost by mistake does not concern my noteholders. The bottom line is that one cannot afford to permit such events without enacting punitive measures. However, you will note that I did NOT call the police, as was within my rights..."

"I did notice. That was kind of you, Hans."

"As stated, Herr Jäger was a virtual son."

**ONE '38 GLOAM,** Peter returned, donned in black; a charge of five minions in-tow.

Mother prepped coffee while Herr Weinberg greeted, Frida's employment having been verbieten years prior.

Tatiana & Shoshana were sent to their room. Beneath the glow of a nightstand's lamp, Tatiana stretched out in bed as her sister fussed over dolls on the floor.

**KISSING A LEATHERED DIGIT** one hour later, Peter bent forwards dimming the light. A cap, tunic & gauntlets shorn were piled atop a bedcorner. Gaping at curls bristling on muscle, Tatiana glanced up to eyelashes bloodied.

Odd tingles stiffened nipples — her vagina immediately warmed. As gentle flicks loosened gownstraps, she studied a ring's grim

face. "Like that, do you? I am an angel now
and Death is my god."

A silver eagle unbuckled. Snores drifted up
from the rug. "Peter...please...kill her first."

The naked form shrugged with indifference.
"Why? Do you not feel love for your sister?"

A Luger was lain in her palm.

"YO SPACECASE — WAX IN THE EARS?"

Wally Good thwacked rump.

"Sorry...I'm sorry. What is it now?"

"Said: forgot to tellya — the Coals invited us for grub
next Tuesday! That jake by you?"

"But...the Colds? Who are 'The Colds'?"

"Eh, just some goon from work and his creepyass
wife. Didn't wanna be rude — I said yeah, okay?"

"Sure, Wally. Sure. It will be nice to be social.
But...but where did your kumpel run off to?"

Shrugging, Wally Good defilmed fresh Camels.

"Got me. Tossed him a fin to score us
some reefers goin' on like an hour ago."

**LESTER WAS THRILLED** to witness his sponsor
swiftly knit tight with Cornell.

The trio soon resembled a family-unit.

Generosities continued to flow; the fat man quashing
bills unpaid, purchasing a Westinghouse television,
outfitting each brother with vast formal wardrobes.
He'd even treated them to a night at Broadway's JACK
DEMPSEY'S — where the exchampion had greeted
Lester beneath flaming neonic stutters.

"Quite the dapper little chap, ain'tcha then?"

"Yessir."

"An' whatcha gonna have ya tonight? Got us

a swell Porterhouse here!
Like ya some steaks, boy?"
"No, sir — want me some catfish."
The exchampion winked at Lester's escorts.
The fat man beamed sad pride.
"Sorry boy, we don't serve-up no catfish!"
Glancing down to patent toecaps, Lester studied twin
frowns. The patronization of a white lummox burned
— no matter the width of its sleeves.
"How's 'bout I letcha sock me one instead?"
Hands upon hips, the exchampion grinned, thrusting
forth a potbelly. "Kay, boy — do your worst!"
Brows furrowed, feet anchored, Lester swung for the
fences. As a tiny fist vanished atop Dempsey's groin,
the exchampion sank with dismay.

**EVERY OUNCE OF RESERVE** was spent keeping
strip-mum — only jinxfears preventing exuberant
fissures. Internally though, Jack Coal's berth on Cloud
Nine remained firmly affixed.
A buzzer shrilled.
"Get that, dear? Still doing my face!"
A door's crack revealed a bluesmokey squint. Greasy
leather. Inksmeared denim. A guitar dangling from
twine. Least he shaved, thought Jack Coal — both
vexed & amused by notions of spousal-disgust
as a large paper sack was thrust forwards.
"Glad you could make it, chum! And what's this?"
Still clogging the jamb, bending slightly,
Jack Coal spied a hallway forsook.
"Just me. Tots ain't comin'. That's kugel. She made it."
"Now that's a darn shame — Dot was really looking
forward to some good/old-fashioned chinwag! You

know how these hens love to squawk!"

Ignoring a wink, awaiting the threshold to clear, Wally Good purged a damp butt to the mat.

**DOT FLITTED ABOUT** the livingroom in a strapless Jack Coal hadn't noted before.

New? Bit snug considering...

He pondered whispering some gentle advice, but she was still keeping her scoop tightvested. He smiled, mulling clandestine fun. Must be bursting at seams! Indeed, they BOTH harbored secrets!

"So...believe you two may've met in passing at the shop the other day, but let's make this bona fide! Dorothy, this is Wallace Good — young fella I've told you so much about!"

Dot nodded once. "Nice to meetcha, Wallace! Heard nothing but fine things about your work, which is very high praise indeed...Jack's lips are snugger than a Scotchman's purse when it comes to doling out praise."

A glance cast pain. "Now Hon, not so! I compliment you all the time! Fact, I was just thinking you've never looked lovelier once in your life! You...you look radiant! Practically glowing! Say, chum, don'tcha agree?"

A hand lighted atop shoulderpadding, Lips pecked a left jowl. "Relax, dear...just teasing."

Green orbs rolled. She flicked a pink lobe.

"I take it all back, Wallace! Dreamboat here is the choicest husband in history!"

**METHODICALLY CHIPPING** mounds of beef, Wally Good forced a wan smile

"Swell chow, Mrs. Coal. Really first-rate."

"Thank you, Wallace."

"Please. Goody is fine."

"Well, thank you...GOODY. Methuselah here's
a big fan of my pot-roast too..."

A fork waved a gristly grey flag.

"So then...where's your wife? I was so looking forward to us meeting tonight! She's foreign, I'm told?"

"German, yeah. Teaches dancin' Tuesdays. Couldn't
reschedule, but sends her deepest regrets."

A jubilant clap stirred dust.

"Oh! I simply ADORE dancing! Jackie & I used to
cut rugs at least thrice weekly — we were a couple
of regular jitterbuggers!"

"Ah, this ain't nothin' like that. It's...it's folkdancin'."

"I'm sorry? 'Folkdancing'?"

Shielding with linen, Wally Good belched.

"Yeah. Ethnic stuff. Y'know, dances from all over the
world. Mostly Europe, but some Western too."

"Western? Do you mean like squaredancing?"

"Pretty much. That's actually how we got tangled, at
a hoedown. We had hangar-hoohahs Saturday nights.
Army was lousy with hayseeds..."

"Oh! How lovely! Dear, imagine that!
Squaredances in Germany!"

Chewing the thought, Jack Coal shrugged.

"Who'da thunk it? They use accordions in lieu of
banjos? Gotta cop to being part-hillbilly myself — my
pa played a wicked spoons! Had his own jug-outfit
and everything! THE OLDE KING COAL BAND!
Hmph...reckon such talent's genetic?"

As utensils spat gravy from a left palm,
green eyes broadcast chagrin.

**SCANNING GRIM MIENS,** Estes Kefauver curtly
dephlegmed before rapping a small oaken gavel.

"This meeting of the Senate Subcommittee Investigating Juvenile Delinquency will now be in order. Today and tomorrow, this committee — of which I chair — is going into the problem of horror & crime comic books. By comic books, we mean pamphlets illustrating stories depicting crimes or dealing with horror. We shall not be talking about the predominantly wholesome comic STRIPS that appear daily in most of our newspapers — and we shall be limiting our investigation solely to those titles dealing with crime & horror. Thus, while there are more than a billion comics sold in the United States each year, our focus remains upon only a fraction."

Hunched atop a backroom bench, Millard Gaines sucked a small carton. His bottle's depletion two days prior had triggered a state of near-ruin. Noting tripodded orthicons — he silently prayed the cameras served solely documentarian purposes.

"While authorities agree that the majority of comics are as harmless as sodapop, hundreds of thousands of horror & crime titles are peddled to young ones of impressionable ages. Examples of types to which we refer have been brought to this hearing for personal attention. I wish at this time to emphatically state that freedom of the press is NOT at issue here. This committee's members...Senator Hannoch, Senator Hennings & myself...are fully aware of the long, hard, bitter fight that's been waged to achieve and preserve such liberties — as well as the other freedoms in our Bill of Rights which we all so dearly cherish. We are NOT a committee of blue-nosed censors. We simply

want to find out what DAMAGE, if any, is being done
to young minds by publications which contain
a substantial degree of sadism."

**A FLASHBULB'S MISFIRE** setting tweed
ablaze forced a ten-minute recess. Paramed-
ics of deadpan comportments removed a
form blistered & steaming. Estes Kefauver
resumed tieskewed — intermittently slapping
a buzzing horsefly that'd somehow breached
the windowless room.

"Since last November, this committee's been holding
public-hearings into facets of the juvenile delinquency crisis that's been correctly labeled America's
Shame. Should this tide continue to swell, by 1960
more than one & a half million American youngsters
will be in trouble with the law each year. Our committee is seeking to determine just WHY so many young
Americans are unable to adjust to lawful patterns of
society...why more & more are turning to nihilism,
crime & narcotics. Though this increase in craven acts
is rising at a frightening pace, we know that the great
mass of our children are not lawbreakers...that even
the majority of those who DO get into trouble are
not criminal by nature. Nevertheless, more & more
are engaging in serious offenses. Our committee is
seeking ways & means to check this trend, to reverse
this youthful crimepattern. We're perfectly aware
that there are no simple solutions to such a complex
problem. We acknowledge that what makes this pickle
so complex is its myriad contributing factors. Therefore, while it would be WRONG to assume that crime
& horror comics are the main fuel of delinquency's

engine — it would be just as erroneous to categori-
cally state that they have no effect whatsoever. From
mail received, we're aware many parents are greatly
concerned about detriments forced upon children.
We firmly believe they have a RIGHT to more knowl-
edge...to know just who's producing this stuff...to
know how such an industry functions..."

Inhaling deep, Millard Gaines cringed. The
room tasted of tea brewed within
a scorched tin cauldron.

**AN ACNE-FRAUGHT BOY** rapped a glass door
barking MISTER JOHN COAL — who tipped the
youth a full quarter despite fastmounting angst. He'd
received only two telegrams since leaving PA — one
heralding his sheepdog's quietus, the other that of his
father. If Western Union was not Death's angel, it was
surely some form of cousin.

Fleeing the workspace, he ferried downhall to the
floor's communal toilet; tears over a maternal-demise
were certainly best shed in private. Shifting a bolt,
inspiring fumes, he scanned walls greasepenciled.

Leonore Silvian puts out for rum —
call MU8-3634!
I LIKE KIKE
*dull old coal mulled the pole of a foal*
Helen Gahagan Douglas just
LOVES the negro people! !

Above a crusty porcelain tank, Christine Jorgensen
and The Apparition fornicated beside a mason jar
housing brined organs. Though the scrawl was inscribed WILL MEISER, Jack Coal assessed its au-
thenticity dubious. Glancing down to the envelope, he

unfolded a '32 Olympics **penknife.**
-DEAR-MR.COAL-DOTTY&ME-ACCEPTED-MOVING-FOR-
WARD-PLEASE-DELIVER-SIX-WEEKS-OF-DAILIES-AT-EAR-
LIEST-CONVENIENCE-EXPECT-STANDARD-CONTRACT-
SHORTLY-WARD-GREENE-KING-FEATURES-SYNDICATE-

**BENEATH A GLOW JAUNDICED,** fingers aquiver, Jack Coal staked five hundred looksees before vertigo finally struck. Coming to, dousing jowls with water, he browsed five hundred times more.

He slapped himself. Once. Thrice. Two dozen times.

Grimy floorchecks were surveyed; black & white tiles shellacked by dried urine — stippled via timefrozen insect. He grinned down to creased Florsheims. Soon they'll be cordovan Westons. Leaning over, tightening laces, sweatslickened spectacles plunged.

**GLIDING BACK, STUDIOBOUND,** a dire mien was assumed. A roomful of drama-parched biddies were about to receive a good show! He'd wail over a mother's sad end — detongued by a concupiscent yegg — awaiting the very last leercollapse before blasting Prosperity's hose!

He heard congrats, felt slaps, witnessed Mesier's proud tears! He pondered a box of Havanas.

Eh..joint's smoky enough as-is.

**ASTONISHED TO ENTER** a nearempty shop, Jack Coal sighed whilst moist eyes perused a missive proffered. "G-g-g-glad your m-m-m-mother's n-n-n-not d-d-d-dead..."

An Underwood dinged from the bald man's office — a brunette returned a blank gape.

"Edna — where the heck IS everybody?"

Shrugging, the secretary molarcracked gum before recommencing to pound. "Aw, they all went down to some saloon...watchin' the bossman testify...least somethin' like that, I think...s'on the teevee... g'wan...join 'em...I ain't gonna squeal..."

"Testify? TV? What's THAT all about?"

Again, a shrug.

"Dunno. Nobody tells me nothin' round here..."

**JACK COAL HOVERED** for five minutes more while the typewriter clattered & clanged. Lips pursed as a platen deleafed. "Sure you can see through them busted specs, hon? Maybe run home'n grab spares?"

Ninety six Ednas cracked gum.

**STAIRCLIMBING SOILED & SLOW,** Lester and Stella broadcast torpor. Five postratting hours had been whiled scouring wireracked troves.

ASPHYXIATION

MARCH OF CRIME

THRILLING DEATH

YARNS OF LAWBREAKING SUSPENSE

Atop the sheaf, a négligéed blonde shrank from a tramp's grisly platter. "I know yer mute, Miss Caitlin — but even if you COULD yell, them folks yonder can't call no cops! Lookee here... done already hacked-out their tongues!"

Sighing rueful, coiling pulp, Lester buried the scene in a pocket. With the advent of recent newsreports, Cornell had insatiably censored. Others could serve as decoys, but he wouldn't surrender this one.

**TWO TIERS YET SCALED,** Stella growled then wailed — hacking as Lester's pace failed.

"S'wrong, boy? Why so rushy?
Ain't be no rats up there!"

Reaching their floor, Stella scratched the door, goug-
ing thick green slather. Deshirting a rusty ballchain,
Lester groped to brassgather. Ramming a crack, the
poodle absconded, her new master's key still lock-
bound — choking both 'til a leash was forsook.

Downhall blared an agonized sound.

**NUDE SAVE AN IVORY SINGLET,** the scholar
stood in wide-eyed shock. Kneeling beneath, fat flesh
flared red as fangs gnashed a floral cravat.

"Get...her...off! Can't...breathe! Killing...me!"

As Lester stooped to wrench the tangle, his face met
a turgid pole. The purple erection was veiny & large —
slick with viscous fresh drool. Rearing back, vising a
firm poodle-torso, he tugged with all his young might;
yanking the fat man free of perched knees —
forcing a violent floorsmite.

Stella shook a pink scrap.

Her victim rolled gasping.

Cornell's member bobbed with each yell.

"YOU JUST GO FOR A WALK RIGHT NOW,
YOUNG MAN! KNOW WHAT THAT SHOELACE
MEANS DAMNWELL!"

**FLEEING THE CARNAGE,** swiping strange spit,
Lester trailed Stella's swift gait. As he searched a glass
knob for a missing hi-sign, sobs distant rattled thin
pine. Good...SHOULD be cryin'!

Hope that big ugly thing gag him to death!

Halfway to the roof, Lester paused then cussed.

He'd abandoned three new finds on the floor.

Now Cornell would toss 'em for sure.

**SENATOR HENNINGS,** fifty four & wide,
jabbed a magnified board.

"And what do you have to say about that?"

Studying panels through thick bifocals, Millard Gaines eyerubbed. Without his drug, the world screamed schmaltz — no matter how thorough lenses were polished.

"Well...I'd say they got what they deserved."

The wide man clucked a pale tongue.

"And this is one of YOUR series? Parents frying in the electric-chair while their child cackles & yuks?"

A grin curled beneath faint beads. "Yes."

"And as we understand from Doctor Wertham's testimony, this little girl is TRIUMPHANT?"

"Listen, sir...if I may explain...the readers don't know that until the very last panel! One of the things we try to do is give each ending an O.Henry twist. We take great pride in our writing..."

A pencil bounced against the wide man's lips. Millard Gaines pined nicotine too.

"That's very nice, your pride! It's a very noble thing to take PRIDE in one's work! But let's stick to the topic... in your opinion, would the average reader be led to believe that this child emerges as some kind of moral SUPERIOR by 'framing' her mother and father?"

"Well, if you'd actually enlarged the FIRST six pages, you'd see that the child leads a life of abject abuse! It's only on the last page she snaps..."

"But what you're essentially feeding us here is that her TRIUMPH is a byproduct of PERJURY?"

Millard Gaines sucked dry foam.

"Yeah...yessir...that's right."

"And that this vengeance is the 'O. HENRY' wrap from which your aforementioned pride duly stems?"

"Yes."

The pencil bounced thrice more.

"Do you think such morality does readers good?"

"No sir, don't think it does them one LICK of good... but neither do I think it causes much harm! It's just a comic book story...escapism...no more, no less... just like movies or television...it's not MEANT as an educational tool! There certainly ARE comics that promote such things, but this particular story isn't one of them! It exists solely to provides stimulation..."

"Interesting choice of words."

**LUNCH WAS COFFEE AT WOOLWORTH'S —** seasoned with benniesoaked wads.

Three cracked inhalers later, Millard Gaines felt a million bucks. Upon the hearing's re-convention, he looked like $1,000,000 too; the benzedrine pairing with sleep-deprivation to imbue a waxy green pallor.

"Gentleman, I'm here as a voluntary witness. You didn't have to subpoena me — I asked for and was given this chance to be heard."

Pausing to attend any forthcoming queries, shot eyes glanced benchwards.

"Two decades ago, my late father was instrumental to this industry's birth...and he was darn proud of his baby! His labors brought joy to thousands world-wide...employment to hundreds of craftsmen! It's weaned children from pictures-to-words, essentially teaching literacy! It's stirred imaginations and provid-ed escape...and, most importantly, entertainment! Yes, my father was proud! He was a pioneer, ahead of his time...the first to produce educational comics! HE-MEN OF SCIENCE! HEROIC WORLD HISTORY! MOSES & HIS MAGICAL STAFF! **Here...**"

As Millard Gaines withdrew a stack from his case, Estes Kefauver fingered a bailiff's attention. "These will be received for the permanent files. Let that be...exhibit eleven. Sir, you may proceed."

"Thank you. Anyway, since '42 — we've sold more than five million copies of MOSES in dozens of lingoes. It's used worldwide to make religion seem vivid & real. But...despite this success...MOSES is still nothing more than a comic! I publish many other titles in addition to MOSES — for instance, a plethora of horror! I was the FIRST publisher to produce horror comics...I'M responsible, I started 'em! Some may not approve of my products, but I contend it's all a matter of taste...it'd be just as tough to explain harmless thrills to a Wertham as LOVE to a frigid old maid!"

Millard Gaines coughed; not to breach any phlegmatic gridlock, but to quell a tide of raw indignation — a gesture largely in vain.

"Yes! My father was PROUD of his comics, and I'm proud of MY comics too! We use the best writers & the finest artists! We spare nothing to make each page an honest-to-goodness work of art! The comic book is the only pleasure Joe Schmoe can buy for a dime...and darn it if PLEASURE ain't my middle name! Entertainment! Reading enjoyment! Entertaining reading is incapable of harming a fly! When Federal Judge Woolsey lifted the ban on ULYSSES, he said, 'It's only with normal people that the law is concerned.'

May I repeat: IT'S ONLY WITH NORMAL PEO-
PLE THAT THE LAW IS CONCERNED! **Young
Americans are normal children! Congenitally altruis-
tic & bright! But those who seek to prohibit & censor
seem to view our youth as dirty, sneaky, perverted
morons using comics as blueprints for action! But
perverted morons are few & far between! They don't
read comics and chances are most dwell in retard-asy-
lums anyway! So...what're we all so very AFRAID
of? Do we fear our own children? Do we forget that
they're, in fact, citizens too? Are they not entitled to
select what to read on their own? Do we think them
so imbecilic that mere cartoons will inspire a legion of
Capones? Jimmy Walker once remarked that he never
knew a girl ruint by a book! Well...I contend nobody's
ever been ruint by a COMIC! A child's personality
is chiseled by three — a magazine can't transform
lambs to sharks & certainly the flipside is true! The
germs of pathologies burrow much deeper! The truth
is that delinquency stems from environments — not
from the fiction one reads! No pill can cure juvenile
delinquency! No law will legislate it out-of-being! Its
roots are economic & social! Its victims need compas-
sion & kindness — not Francoesque bowdlerizers! It's
affection they need! Decency! Nutrition! Substance!
Gentlemen...distinguished senators...once you begin
to censor, even a little, you'll soon find yourself censoring everything! Books! Radio! Television! Papers!
Next, you'll be censoring what people SPEAK...even to
themselves atop toilets!"**

Silence blanketed the room — only an odd
buzz could be heard. Acutely aware of a na-

tion's trained orbs, Millard Gaines struggled to disregard anal burns. He wondered if the committee was likewise hemorrhoidal.

He certainly hoped that they were.

**THE AIR WAS CHILLY** up on the roof.

Pigeons bobbed alongst bricks. Vising Stella's lead, Lester sighed. "My brotha...he...he a fairy..."

Bob Fujitani's face screwed. "Gee, whatcha mean fairy? Kinda like in PETER PAN?"

"Nah...he...he like otha boys. That mean fairy too..."

"So, what's wrong with that? I like boys! I mean, hey — don't I like YOU?"

Lester lobbed a Pepsi-cap. A scatter squawked avian hexes. "Ain't the same...he be a fairy...head funny..."

"Gee...that's too bad, Les. My big brother croaked in the camp — least yours ain't pushin' daisies."

As Lester slumped, limp as a rag, his best friend probed Stella's wool. Straining towards a flock resettled, canine-joints writhed tauter than steel.

"So, does that mean you'll be funny too someday?"

"Dunno...could be...hope not..."

"Gee whiz, I surely hope not too."

"Lester?"

"Yeah?"

"Gotta tellya something."

"Okeh."

Recalling sputum, Bob Fujitani glanced sunwards for strength. "My mom says we can't play anymore..."

Lester examined three rolling bulges distorting his companion's striped tee. "Whatchu mean?"

"She says...that...that you're a bad boy..."

"Huh? Bad boy why fo'? Ain't no badder than you!"

Stella pounced atop a passing cockroach.

"Shit, know that..."

"Then why don'tcha say nothin'? I ain't so bad."

"I did, Les! Told her just that...but she just shook her head and said no...that you're a really bad boy..."

"She mean BLACK boy."

"Yeah...I know. Maybe."

Craning southeast towards Wall Street peaks, Lester mulled bullets & steeples. "But...but that don't make no danged sense! Mean...you...youse kin all Chinee!"

"Japanese!"

"Don't make no diff'rence! Yo' mama think she betta than niggas, but she ain't! Nightriders string her up fast as any ol' coon! Someday, maybe, you see..."

"Jeepers, hope not! I love my mom...
even if she does see SOME things cockeyed..."

"Well...whatchu gon' do? Gon' act like she want?"

Laughs forced dropped like turds.

"Think I'd do my best pal like that?"

"Yeah...guess we jus' gon' hafta see..."

Resting a palm atop a sloped shoulder, Bob Fujitani squeezed. "Aw, don't be like that, Les! I'm your pal to the end! All the way! Straight down the line!"

"Oh — so we's pals to the end, huh?"

"That's what I said, didn't I?"

Honing focus upon Trinity's spire, withdrawing a gold Remington folder, Lester thrust a right hand forth. Dusklight danced across 'Butchie'.

"Reckon y'know what bloodbrotha mean."

Bob Fujitani breathed smog.

**RETURNING TO HARLEM,** Dr. Wertham
slumped, mulling Californian vacations — two days
spent in a Federal hearing warranted a month's worth
of rest. Lowering a forehead to arms deskfolded,
he drifted across dreamless black syrup.

An intercom razzed, dipteric & cruel.

"There's a Mrs. Fuentes here."

"But does she have an appointment, Cora? Did we
not already establish today's preoccupation?"

"But...sir...she's very upset."

"Have we not repeatedly addressed unannounced
visitations with enough ample conviction?"

"I'm sorry — she says you've met prior.
It's her son, sir...he's in trouble..."

Scratching a nose, palming soft hoar, the old man
stood and then sighed. "Send her in."

**MASCARAED EYES** topped silk bosomed near-
bust. "Sorry Doc, didn't know where else to go..."

Digits twirled glossy jet curls.

"Please — have a seat."

Lifting a file, the old man recalled a handsome
young face supporting three inches of grease.

"And what is your favorite comic, Luis?"

"HUMAN TORTURE."

"You mean 'HUMAN TORCH', do you not?"

"No...H U M A N   T O R T U R E!"

A throat hacked once.

"Luis Grisóstomo Fuentes — age nine. Sleeps in
one bed with a brother, eleven. Claims his father was
killed as a Minnesota logger. Mother reveals that the
man has, in fact, overdosed via narcotics. Gestures
wildly as he describes crimes he enjoys. Tells me,

'Strangling is the cat's meow, I consider it my favorite pain. I like the Phantom & his magic skull-ring, he is the angel of death. And Shining Knight too because his horse flies. This world ain't nothing but garbage, how I yearn to watch it all burn.'"

"That's him. Pinched again. Switchblade this time. Desk-sergeant says it was all scabby and bent."

"And Luis attributed such gore to whom?"

Soft shoulders shrugged.

"Just says it's the blood of a rat."

**SOBS DIVULGED** a shelter's squalor.

"And then they said I should be glad he ain't up in Warwick...that shit's way much worser in there!"

Old digits scrawled in tandem with tears, notating assorted shortcomings. But decent...hardworking...provides the best care she can. Alas, sometimes even one's BEST is deficient.

"Please, Mrs. Fuentes...compose yourself...do not despair! With proper guidance, there remains hope yet! Tomorrow morning, I will make some calls.
Your son shall be duly released!"

Leaning deskwards, exposing breasts mashed, the plush woman gazed deep & long.

"Oh Doc...such a saint...nothin' I can do in return?"

Beneath magnified blues, fingers whiskbroomed.

"Ach...you may leave."

**PITSTOPPING ALONGST SECOND AVE,** Jack Coal purchased one dozen pink roses — the cowled monger's pushcart a'hop whilst a rusty kukri hacked stems. Lips arched north as feet scraped, the rustling mass reeling reverie a hazy score prior.

To the dawn of a quest to inkdouse New York.
Dragging Dot kicking & screaming.
Lean years. Walkups on C.
Rents of fifty eight bucks.
He'd rounded each syndicate so pertina-
ciously receptionists ceased offering seats. A
razor grew dull. Soles bore holes. Pants
took on sickening shines.
Suppers — sardines on toast.

**DESIDERATA'S FLAMES** waning hope to
steam forced Jack Coal rungs lower; base
onepanelers for stagmagazines — unabashed,
freewheeling smut. Ignorant of carnality's
rogues, he'd relied upon Dot's cackles for
source; a maiden PEEP'N'PANT sale funding
a celebratory jumbo-bouquet.
    "Christ, Jack — what were you thinking?"
    "But hon, y'always say pink's better'n red."
    "You big dope...I was talking 'bout STEAKS!"

**BENEATH OTIS-GLOWS,** orbs strained through
fissures — cringing upon the sight of browned petals.
    Bilked! Hoodwinked by a lecherous wop!
He briefly pondered reversing the lift, but quickly
dismissed this notion. Life was too short — once Dot
learned of the new strip, petty trifles would bail.
Now was a time to discuss crucial things.
    Connecticut...sheepdogs...Junior!
    Yes, by golly'll just bring it up myowndarn-
self! Why should I wait any longer?
    Had a man no right to discuss such things?
    Especially one mining BUSHMILLER ducats?
    Perhaps, **he thought,** she's simply AFRAID?

Maybe thinks I don't want kids anymore?
That I've grown too used to having my space?
Perhaps fears I'd even be cross?

Hardly unreasonable assumptions —
years had lapsed devoid of such bandy.

Can't let misunderstandings corrupt her
peace! Gotta set things straight!

Lilting Porter to a mic floral, gamboling alongst the
tenth floor, a mashed Camel-dreg froze whirls.

**STOOPING, SNIPING THE BUTT** — Jack Coal
doorflattened an ear. Detecting naught,
he fed the lock; rotating silent & slow.

The lights were dimmed in the livingroom. An amber blur disrupted the couch. Traversing the gap
upon tiptoes, taps soft coaxed steel hums.

Goblets chimed from the bedroom.

"And how's it going with ol' Willie?"
. "Eh...okay, I guess."

"Shrewd little kike, bet he's squeezing you
dry...talented twerp like yourself. Keep your
eyes sharp. Watch your back. He's not okay —
he's GARBAGE!"

"He ain't that bad. Anyway...don't say kike."

"And you're CERTAIN Jack's at the bar with
the boys? Doesn't sound much like him."

"Gone when I left...so yeah...guess so.
Mean, one'a the boys too, ain't he?"

"Well, sort of. And why's Willie on the TV?"

"Fuck knows? Long as my pay's
ontime, I give two shits."

Behind cracked webs, lids clamped.

**YAWNING BILIOUS,** temples clutched, a rubber skull tickled graymatter as shards rained atop carpet.

In the foyer lurked an antique rolltop purchased many years prior. Though it's cost had exceeded fifty pages, the smile it'd planted across lips red was undoubtedly worth sixty more. Tissues strained to wrench ebony slats gummed & slightly offtrack.

This is fixable. This is not beyond repair.

Sliding open a far right drawer, groping blind for spares, elastic fingers brushed something soft and coiled like five hungry snakes. A chamois bag was slowly withdrawn; then came a cardboard box. Darting in for a third time — steel rims finally emerged.

Muffled moans pursued springcreaks.

A dangling sack aped a pistolshaped scrotum.

Sheathing the desk, spinning with purpose, Jack Coal paused then quaked. No! Not the solution...

is JUNIOR not trapped in there too?!!

Burying paternal-souvenirs in a coatpocket, lifting the flawed bouquet, he slithered out the frontdoor.

**PEERING THROUGH SMOKE** at a stern squint, Dot traced a creased forehead.

"Did you just hear something? Some kinda slam?"

"Nope. Nah, just you."

"Say, do you play golf?"

"In Minnesota we throw axes...why?"

"Not a trap. Knitted Methuselah some headcovers for Christmas, but it's been ages since he's hit the links."

**ROOF-ENSCONCED** despite a friend's dash, Lester pondered mephitic Oriental concoctions; feet static despite bellyaches. Corny just gon' whup me.

Surveying moonsilver, he pined for the South — how

he HATED New York. Folks ain't right in they's heads up here. The yanks were even dumber than spooks; the chinamen — exceedingly worse.

He glanced down to an aching left palm.

A gash caked with burgundy crust.

Scabs half-Jackson/half-Fujitani.

His lips had kept mum as ichor'd hopped veins — despite spying a shoelaced wrist — the familial heartbreak of a nigger-infusion was fair retribution enough.

Lester wasn't cross with his friend, who hadn't known any better. Nor with Cornell, or even the fat man. Lester was angry with God.

Recalling the pocketlodged comic, he shoved Stella clear of his lap.

**MISTLETOE SPRIGS & STYROFOAM SNOW** framed palms stabbing Lionel stubble. Above bakelite fronds, a tin DC-7 spun from a waxy white string. Beyond the diorama, a postered sunburst was ruptured by a porpoise's jubilant leap.

SAN DIEGO — WHERE CALIFORNIA BEGAN!

Leaning transfixed, face glassmashed, Jack Coal pulsed burdens of shame. He'd been a greedy, callous, stupid man. This was entirely all his OWN fault!

But...CALIFORNIA!

Lands golden & fertile! Should've brought her there in the FIRST place!

Why then had he dragged those sweet rosy cheeks to this consarned cesspool instead? To despair. Dismay. Degeneracy. Lice, blood, rape, warts, decay, maggots, tumors & rats. Was it any WONDER that twenty years of exposure might leave her somewhat...tainted?

But it's not too late! I can fix it!
None of this is beyond repair!
Were things not verging on CHANGE?
Was he not resilient? Flexible?
Rife with powers newfound?

He saw Dot rumping a backdoor's screen — grasping laundry sundried, ferrying freshplucked oranges atop.

A belly was swollen nearglobe.

He could taste the flesh of young fruit.

Something sharp pinched his right lobe. Wincing, he spun — spitting frost. A lesionous blonde smiled expectantly, waving towards a dangling bouquet.

"Stretch, dem pretties dere all just for me?"

He studied the creature, immobile & blank. Dark roots...a throat's peachpit...an inexplicably familiar air.

Words brawny cast rank bleach.

"On account ya stiffed me last time?"

Staggering off, Jack Coal fled — strides extending with each fading shriek. Two blocks on, a larcenous gale displaced his hat sixty yards. Swiveling fluid, groping grotesque, the Stetson was plucked from an iron lamppost irradiating a Chock Full O'Nuts.

**SQUINTING MIDGLOAM,** decrypting fonts Leroy, a story entitled THE UNKILLABLE BEAST bored Lester to nigh-abandon. Yet another ray-drenched scientist had become a misshapen hulk.

Mulling a homestead-return, he wondered how upset his brother might be now that he'd spied his bare john-son. He processed the quandary long & hard before concluding Cornell would likely say nothing.

Glancing down, he grinned at Stella — who'd patiently awaited his notice. A tail thumped.

"Aw...y'hungry?"
She whimpered sweetly.
"Want ya some food, boy? Fetcha some rats?"
Rising tall atop legs hind, the poodle showed off for
her hero — pirouetting, backflipping thrice.
Orbs brown spied pupilglazed moons.
"This all be YO' fault...y'know that, right?"
An adoring tongue lapped hands agrope,
pants heaving as arms firmed skywards.
Gauging the ledge, Lester sighed. "Love y' too, boy.
Have a nice trip." Summoning might, he threw.

**JAGER'S BAR & GRILL** was an underlit tavern
with a decor some would describe as Black Forest.
Relieved to be its sole customer, Jack Coal requested
three pickled-eggs. A minute further, he ordered five
more — feeling though he might scarf a thousand.
A mug of draught was set before him.
He'd not asked for a beer — but was nonetheless
pleased by its presence; it was exactly what he re-
quired. Downed in one gulp, a second was poured.
The bartender...tall, middleaged, beetlebrowed...eyed
his subject's tired bouquet. Deep, European tones
unwound in recitational-fashion.
"Like that, eh? WURZBURGER! Besides Luchow's,
we are the only bar in Manhattan to serve it."
Fizz-spellbound, Jack Coal belched.
"Yeah, like it. S'good."

**THE EGGS & BEER** worked medicinally, melting
away strife's tautness. Soon, jowls swung freely again.
Glancing up to the bartender's mien, Jack Coal assessed significant creases. This was a man who'd
SEEN things— a man strangers could trust.

Grinning, he wriggled a pointer.

"Say fella, lemme me askya something..."

Lips pursed, tediumbraced.

"...whaddya knows 'bout wimmens?"

Nodding, shrugging, the bartender swiped an already immaculate counter. "As much as any other chap, I suppose. I know that all they respect is money & power. Does THAT answer your question?"

Jack Coal smirked at gleaming woodgrain.

"Ah, I see...you're a romantic."

Lifting a stein, wiping pewter,
the bartender shrugged once more.

"Ach, my life has not been without passion."

Resting the mug, leaning forwards, an accent miraculously wisped: "But m'boy, if there's one thing I know in life — it's people! People and people's troubles! And you, sir, are a PEOPLE with TROUBLES!"

Peering into cyan-rimmed pupils, Jack Coal recoiled from twin Apparitions mulling space within rockets.

"Understood...but what can I do?"

Leaning back, reseizing the stein, the bartender blew spittle and polished. "Ach, there is only one thing TO do, sir — one must beseitigen the source!"

A gun jostled within a topcoat as guitars & blue pencils blitzed vision. Greasy hair. Greasy boots. Arrogant perpetual squints.

**MOTIONING FOR A THIRD BEER,** Jack Coal noted a small, cornermounted TV.

...watchin' the bossman testify...

"Can you put on CBS please?"

Cursorily knobfiddling to descramble reception, the

bartender's hands fell defeated. "Looks like another 'senate hearing' or whatever they call them! Every day, it's this McCARTHY fellow — him or the other...with the silly hat! EVERY DAY! Such busy, IMPORTANT men they are! ACH! Semper Vigilans!"

Puffy bags of sallow flesh anchored a man's sad eyes.

"Earlier today, the subcommittee heard the continued testimony of Doctor Fredric Wertham — a leading exponent of the psychological impact of comic book magazines. Here now is the man in his own words..."

"MISTER SENATORS, I WILL TELL YOU THIS: CHILDREN DO NOT DISLIKE AUTHORITY! ON THE CONTRARY, THEY HAVE A STRONG INNER-URGE TO FIND AND FOLLOW AUTHORITIES WHOM THEY CAN TRUST! THEY MAY NOT ALWAYS UNDERSTAND WHAT IS BEST FOR THEM, BUT THEY CRAVE OUR FIRM GUIDANCE! A LARGE PART OF A CHILD'S INNER-LIFE CONSISTS OF THIS SEARCH FOR AUTHORITATIVE WISDOM, DISCIPLINE & CORRECTION!"

Chuckling, the bartender clapped.

"Wunderbar! Spoken like a true German!"

**OLD GOLDS' GLEEFUL TAPS** ushered Will Meiser's discomfort. "Gentlemen, this industry's long been my primary focus and I've admittedly done quite well by it. Indeed, it's made me a wealthy man! From the start, my intention has been solely to entertain & uplift. And this is what I've done! Entertain! Uplift! It's only within the past several years that disturbing trends have begun to surface. I don't know why...maybe the war's changed appetites... but...nevertheless, the fact remains that the public has come to crave sex & violence in ALL forms of massmedia! The more lurid... the more heinous...the better! At first I resisted, steering clear of such trends — both in my own work and in the books I package for others...I'm fully aware that a great percentage of my readership falls beneath voting-age. However — after intense pressure from advertisers...from distributors...even from my customers themselves — I eventually either had to buckle or face certain bankruptcy. I COULDN'T allow the latter! Not only do I have dependents, my twenty-plus employees all have families of their own! As a result, I have indeed been the source of certain material that I now regret producing. Material from which shame undoubtedly stems."

**A bristly, hornrimmed man jabbed an enlarged illustration. Even through a blizzard of static, Jack Coal recognized** MURDEROUS MORPHINE & I.

**Testes tightened and knotted.**

"Now, Mister Meiser...sir...THIS story...which features narcotic-addiction, smuggling, murder, extortion, kidnapping, prison-escape, rape & suicide...all within nine compact pages...was produced in YOUR studio? Is that correct? Under YOUR watch?"

"Yes...this story was unfortunately a product of my shop and I am indeed FULLY responsible. However, I'd like to point out that it was produced under subcontract and not published beneath my own banner."

"So then...you didn't actually PEDDLE this tripe...but you admit to being its daddy?"

"No sir...the story was employee-produced — drawn by a man named John Coal."

Jotting a ledger, the senator mumbled as cameras zoomed beyond. An easel's lesionous blonde winked at Jack Coal while toilets inhaled his career. His wife, his future, his Packard sank. Junior's cradle spun helplessly past — a mammoth catfish hot on its tail.

**WHILE RISING QUICKLY** eased some pain, crotch-woes duly endured — a scrotum worming in riotous patterns as thumbs belthooked to shift.

"Ach! Such filth! Shameful!"

Teutonic eyes beamed sheer disgust.

"What swine would create such things for DIE KINDER to read? Such a face I would like to see!"

Surveying foam, Jack Coal shrugged.

"A pile of garbage."

A rag's curt slam stirred dregs.

A horsefly dodged strikes further.

"IT'S OFT I WONDER WHY I'VE MOVED TO A NATION FULL OF BLOODSUCKING VAMPIRES!"

**A RIGHT ARM EXTENDED** rippled in long boneless waves. Grasping hands wrenched the limb south.

A frail man stared vested & wan.

"Buddy...how'd ya come to know where I was?"

"I-I-I-I-I c-c-c-can always f-f-f-find you, J-J-J-Jack!"

Spooling thin shoulders ten times around, Jack Coal squeezed unashamed. "S'freezin'! Oughtta be wearing a sweater at least! Gonna catch your death of a cold!"

"S-s-s-saw th-the t-t-teevee, Jack. Awful s-s-sorry!"

"Likewise, chum...me too."

"B-but w-w-where are y-y-you g-g-going n-n-now?"

Digits ricocheted a bulge waistlevel.

"Off to beseitigen some trouble!"

"J-J-J-Jack...d-d-d-don't! Th-th-think of th-th-the ch-ch-children! Th-th-the ch-ch-children will CRY!"

**BOUNCING FREE OF A CHECKER,** Jack Coal caved a stained oaken door. The startled gasp of a receptional Negress was quelled with a waved .44. The Colt chambered verdigrised Bulldogs inherited along with the gun. Ancient board had evanesced to motes as a red box was taxistunned.

Answering thudding caroms, Dr. Wertham was vexed to find a barrel pressing his brow's crease. A swift glance beyond the revolver further compounded this pique — clammy, corpulent, quivering jowls deadrang a behemoth scrotum.

"Sir, kindly state your name and intention; it's been a long day and my patience is thin! I must warn you, if it's MONEY you're after, then you've certainly mischosen your target! I'm merely a physician and not a rich one at that...my efforts are largely pro bono! Herr Rosenblatt nextdoor is a BAIL-BONDSMAN — perhaps it'd be prudent to visit HIM instead!"

Teeth sank into a trembling lip as Jack Coal steadied an arm. Surveilling drops cascading, Dr. Wertham mentally jotted. Contact Sears ASAP to request inexpensive rug-swatches.

"Sir, from the manner in which you brandish this iron — I trust you are not a military-veteran?"

Ambling forward, guntilting a head, Jack Coal en-
tered the office. Traipsing back, Dr. Wertham's blind
steps divulged a danseur's precision.

"Obviously, you're not a conscientious-objector...was
this lack of service based upon something physically
deficient? You certainly appear HEALTHY enough, if
perhaps three stone obese. No...no...wouldn't be that!
Uncle Sam is not so very fussy! Might you have some
kind of NERVOUS disorder, Mister...Mister...?"

"Coal!"

"Mister Cold..."

"That's COAL — you twobit Hitler!"

The chuckling old man nodded.

"Ach, Mister Coal...I'm afraid you've mistaken me for
somebody else! Somebody else entirely! Please allow
me to introduce myself — I am Doctor Fredric Wertham! My immediates were KILLED by the very same
führer whose name you now invoke with such fury! I
no longer even call myself GERMAN — I am as much
American as you! Might you care to survey my
passport? It's here...right in my desk —"

"CAN IT AND REACH FOR THE SKY!"

Palms raised, Dr. Wertham's retreat endured.

"I KNOW EXACTLY WHO YOU ARE, YOU
BLOODSUCKING SWINE, AND I DON'T GIVE A
LEAPIN' LIZARD WHETHER YOU CALL YOUR-
SELF KRAUT...KIKE...YANKEE DOODLE DANDY...
THE CORONATED KING OF SIAM! TO ME —
YOU'RE SIMPLY ONE THING!"

"And this thing is what precisely?"

"TROUBLE!"

Hoary brows fretted north then south.

"CoalCoalCoal...Coal! I don't suppose you might happen to be JOHN Coal, would you? THE John Coal? The famous man of the funnies?"

Darting orbs spied petals crushed within an elbow's arched crook. "While I'm unphased that a man of such...talents...would brandish such a very large pistol, I must admit these ROSES are quite the surprise! It's been eons since I've been courted!"

Shooing blush via glower, Jack Coal gunwagged. "DON'T BE CUTE! GET BEHIND THAT DESK!"

Muttering Deutsch, the old man sat; hands parked on a blotter. Frowning at papers intolerably skewed, he commenced to straighten & tidy.

"So then...Mister Coal...growing quite late now. I must once again request your intentions."

"TO PAINT THIS ROOM WITH YOUR BRAINS!"

"And may I say something before you...redecorate?"

A grunt preceded curt nods.

"Sir, while it's true that I take umbrage with the industry in which you toil — please do not mistake these efforts for character-assassinations! I realize that you are somewhat disturbed, but...please...try to understand...this is NOT about YOU — I simply aim to protect children! Their welfare is paramount!"

"SH-SH-SH-SH-SHUT UP!"

The old man winced then shrugged.

"Now, I realize that you're quite upset...and perhaps you may even have a RIGHT to be — I've undoubtedly wrought your chequebook some harm! But again, I have no interest in ruining careers! This crusade is not financially driven! As you can see, my surroundings are humble! Most of my work is with the desperately poor! There is no profiteering here — my sole reward is the protection of innocents!"

Whites shot welled filmy with dew.

"MY WIFE...SHE THINKS...THINKS I'M A FUCKIN' JOKE! WAS GONNA FIX THIS! WAS GONNA FIX IT! HAVE A NEW LIFE! A SECOND CHANCE! BUT NO! N-NO! Y-YOU! Y-Y-Y-YOU!"

A silver head quaked mournfully.

Dr. Wertham detested Time's waste.

"Mister Coal, please...show some composure! If it helps, be assured that your wife is indeed INcorrect! You are most certainly NOT a joke! Jokes make us laugh! Spread happiness! Deliver joys most profound! You, on the other hand, are NOT funny! You will NOT make us happy! On the contrary, all you imbue is SADNESS! You're a very sick man, I'm afraid! Now then, you ask — is there a cure? Well, while extensive research...much of it my own...has been conducted on hebephrenic schizophrenia, we still have yet to — "

The giant catfish behind the desk babbled further & further. Never before had Jack Coal heard a Siluriformes speak. Nor seen one wear a tie. Nor accrue so many diplomas.

"That is quite an OLD firearm, Herr Coal! A veritable ANTIQUE...are you certain that it still works? Have you disassembled & oiled it...attended its maintenance at all? I myself was a soldier once! Would you care I should help? I might fix it..."

"SHUT UP!"

"Some learned colleagues might even suggest that a gun like that merely substitutes — "

"SHUT UP! SHUT UP! SHUT UP! CAN IT! S-SAVE

THE B-B-BABBLE FOR B-B-B-B-B-B-BELLEVUE!"
Spectacles slid a fleshless wan bridge.
"I'm sorry...Bellevue? I haven't set foot upon those
premises since my tenure ended fifteen years prior..."
"SHUT UP!"
"...the separation was somewhat less than amicable..."
A hammer cocked.
"LAST WORDS, KAPITÄN KATFISH? TIME'S UP!"
The old man placidly smirked.
A soft throat cleared rearwards.
"Mista Wertham...sir...yo' door be broken.
Got dem Thin Mints youse ordered..."
Scowl collapsing in tandem with a pistol's repocket,
the intruder brushed past three uniformed girls.

**DABBING BEADS CLEAR** with a monogrammed
swath, Dr. Wertham grinned upon cookies.
"Thank you, ladies — for making my day!"
The troop's roundest curtsied.
"You welcome, sir. Sorry to innarupt yo' meetin'."
"Don'tchu be sorry none, Eudora — holmes was
plumb rude! Didn't even say hello or goodbye!"
Quietly chewing, the old man paused.
"Maya, I wouldn't take the slight too personally. I
have made a thorough study of Mister Coal's work —
you are quite simply just not his type!"

**RAUCOUS WITH EGGHEADS** & longhairs —
University Place's Cedar Tavern was loud to the
point of distraction. But that was fine...better than
fine...Jack Coal thirsted for every dram of distraction
within the IRT's span! He pounded a double-rye —
an act repeated thricemore.
Awaiting a fifth, an arm girdled his shoulders.

Squinting towards a lingering hand, he noted an odd brassy skull. Had he wandered into a fairybar?

"Whoa, Nellie! Slow it down...ain't BUYIN' tonight!"

The limb's owner squeezed tighter and clucked.

As Jack Coal blinked through spares, whiskyhaze & expired-scripts conspired to unfocus the world — beyond planed bristles and a freckly smear, he simply knew naught what he faced.

"Andrews, pal! Archibald Andrews! Say, put 'er there!" Filching light, the skull gleamed with each bob. "Like that ring? Took it off a dead kraut in ol' Adolf's bunker! I was a paratroop back in Berlin! Rough over there an' how!"

"It's nice."

"Tellya what, pal — treat me an' my friends here a coupla rounds...damned thing's all yours! Swear to Mary! Honest injun!"

A platinum blonde & raven brunette flanked a coat of green plaid. Scalps aside, they broadcast selfsame; in figure, in sweater, in face. Upon nods feeble, the smear barked orders — spying a wallet's emergence.

"Say, thanks pal! Didn't catch YOUR handle!"

"Sorry...Coal. Jack Coal."

Grasping fingers by tips alone, the blonde nimbly shook. "That's Betty — AllAmerican doll!"

A pimp was kicked with an opentoed pump.

Nails were bubblegum-pink.

"Blackie here's Veronica! Watch it, she bites!"

Through a leer feline, the brunette hissed.

Claws flashed beefy lacquer.

"Ladies, meet King Cold — my newest ol' pal!"

"COAL."

"Yessir...that's what I said! Chilly Willy!"
Sidecars were slurped. Glasses were slammed.
Shards scattered in thirty directions.
"Yes! HALLELUJAH! Barkeep — do it again!"
Sucking a finger, twisting & turning, the smear relin-
quished the ring. "Wear it in good stealth!"
The blonde eyed an armcradled bouquet.
"So...who's that for, mister? Yer wifey?"
Jack Coal spied flowers forgotten.
"Nope...strictly for you."
Pert breasts mashing his thorax crushed the blos-
soms betwixt. "Ooh la la...MISTER SMOOTH!"
Petals licked quivering jowls.
"Like dancin', Daddy-O?"
Lobbing roses, wrapping a twenty-inch waist —
Jack Coal yawped as he lifted.
"COME DESDEMONA...LET US NOW SWING!"
 As the pair merged with a shuffling mass, the winking
smear emptied a waxed envelope into a forsaken rye.

**THE OLD MAN'S EVENING** crawled deskencamp-
ed, attending to a backlog. Between the hearing, the
ruckus & its pursuant report — his momentum had
been ramrodded offkilter. Finally departing the clinic
at nine, inhaling crisp Harlem air, he detected pitiful
moans. Atop the lime steps of Saint Phillip's,
Mrs. Fuentes sat shrunk & aquake.

**SWEATDRENCHED** despite frozen temps, Jack
Coal studied moonglows. Obscured by the parkbench
beneath him, rats skittered & fought. How he envied
such beastly lives — untainted by finance or thought.
 Brains ached, fuzz-awash; he wasn't quite sure where
he was. Attempting focus, retracing steps, eyes merely

spun behind lids. Nostrils convulsed. Something rose
from the wool of his suit — an odious vinegarstench.
Rubbing sweat free of a scruff, fingers were held to
a nose. Piss. Fragments hovered: waking supine
beneath a urinal's soffit...a bouncer's choler...
hoofing atop an ancient LaSalle...then —
nothing. THE TIME! What was the time?

Jack Coal flicked a left sleeve. Alas, no Elgin.

A shame. A gift — plated with gold.

Hips were patted. Keys still present...change...
no such luck walletwise. Dot would surely be irked.
Dot...Dot — DOT!

Bolting erect, wrenching a coat, sweat oozed as he
burrowed through pockets. Finding the bulge, he
sighed bittersweet — halfsorry it'd gone undetected.

He'd have to ditch the damned thing himself.

Couldn't be trusted...what if another MOOD struck?

**COFFEE & SCHNAPPS** and an hour's pass
barely dented Hysteria's grasp.

"Ach, my dear...PLEASE...we all do whatever we can!
I know what you've done for this boy! You've tried so
hard — so very hard! You mustn't think it your fault!"

"But Doc, it is! It is! I mean...s'GOTTA be, right?"

**SPYING A PAPERCRAMMED BIN,** Jack Coal
pondered wrapping the pistol like cod.
But what if a tramp were to fish it out?

What if some KID did the same?

He could just toss it into the Hudson...

Walk to the piers, ignoring queers, hurl it right
at the muck. Yessir — that was the ticket.

Arise atop knees unstrung, he collapsed back to the
bench. Head feels funny. Just give it a minute...

Perhaps wounds were best homenursed before resuming plans tomorrow? Reasonable enough...

'Twas precisely this juncture that two shadowcloaked Martians emerged from a dry shrub and leered.

**HIDING BLEARED LASHES,** glancing lapwards, Mrs. Fuentes skirtsmoothed with damp palms.

"Heard it at all the church-sermons! And that judge... he says it too! It's the parents' fault when the children be wrong...he told me that's always the bottomest line, where the buck always stops! I asked him if maybe when he was young...maybe he fucked-up once too..."

"And how did his honor reply?"

"Said NUH-UH — 'cause his parents be good!"

Weary head shaking sadly, the old man kneaded soft shoulders. "Mrs. Fuentes, please, cease this manner of thought — it is stupidity and you are not dumb! You've done everything for Luis within your power! His chart indicates that you've provided this boy a good home! What you must understand is that even a GOOD home's influence can be thwarted by untoward exposure! These comic books, teevee-crime & other such nonsense...these are the REAL enemy! We KNOW good parents when we see them — so enough with these worries and doubts!"

**THE QUEER WHITE HULK** upon the parkbench was a mass of odd tics & dried urine.

Zealous selfslaps set jowls awobble.

Midway through a Catfish-themed rant, Bob Fujitani swirled the CRAZY hi-sign.

Palming its face, digits latticed, the hulk howled through fissures. "Oh Wally! WALLY! So handsome! So virile! I so ADORE a high forehead!"

Through widening gaps, captors were spied.

"If you're lookin' for our leader, head south on the Turnpike then go straight roughly five hours! Can't miss it — big white house — Marines picnicking all over the lawn! The chief is the big baldy with martinibreath!"

Lester's throat cleared. "Um, mista...is you okay?"

Hands dropping, cringe unfurling, a mien gaped fluid & slack. "Golly...you Martians are MUCH less scaly than advertised! Why, you almost look like a coupla regular kids! Very clever! Clever indeed! Borderline diabolic!"

Bob Fujitani espied gleams brass.

"Say, mister — what's that?"

Raising a pointer, brows aloft, the hulk waggled with glee. "Why — that's my ol' lodge-ring! I'm the Grand Goobagobble in Goodstanding of the Society of Syphilitic Simps! Hearda us? We stage the Annual Battery Park Beavereat every third July ninth! Come down sometime! We accept ya! No hymies allowed — but Martians are jake by us!"

Ignoring the hulk's petering rave, the bloodbrothers convened in a huddle. "Hey Martians! Either ya fellas want this here ring? S'all yours if so!"

**HALFWAY THROUGH A JAMB**, Mrs. Fuentes paused. "Doc, sorry to be such a pain — but can ya please tell me once more?"

"Tell you WHAT precisely?"

Breasts quivered responsive to whispers.

"That none of this ain't really my fault."

**UPON MUCH COAXING**, the skull slid free —
its wake leaving a phantasmic green smudge.

"Here y'go, Emperor Jones — my gift to you!"

Plucking the ring from a palm outstretched, rotating eyelevel beamdrenched, Lester smirked while his cohort scowled. "No fair! Didn't give nothing to me!"

Surveying the kvetch, the hulk chinstroked.

"You, sir, are DIRECT! Real straightshooter — a trait to respect & admire!"

A revolver was thrust forth by its barrel.

"Here y'go, pard. Think ye can wield it? Will ye know what t'do when the bell tolls?"

Black hands grabbed at a sleeve.

"No! No! Leave it be!"

An irked arm wrested away.

"Why? You yella? Like some kind of fairy?"

A rat scrambled past Lester's Keds.

"SOME KIND OF FAIRY LIKE CORNY?"

The pausing rodent's tiny tongue razzed.

"Mister, can I really keep this?"

"Course, pard! Gratis! Free! My gift to ye! Jes promise to keep them rattlers a'hoppin'!"

Accepting the Colt, gauging its heft, the small boy took steady aim. "Little Martians — I have here in my hand a list of two hundred & five! A list of names that were made known to the Secretary of Shit as being members of the Garbage Party...who nevertheless are still shaping turdpatties within our own Shit Department!"

"BOBBY...NO — DON'T!"

**COLORFUL PULP FANGVISED,** Michael Rat
scurried breakneck. This was a very good find indeed.
His wife would be beyond thankful!

In celebration, they'd mate at least ten times — perhaps even twenty or thirty; for not only was this paper
a fine insulator, it was utterly ogre-juice drenched.

Previously when Michael had encountered such nec-
tar, it'd been in the form of untransportable droplets,
forcing immediate onsite-laps and accusations of cock
& bull later — Minerva & the children laughing riot-
ously while he'd sulk like a fool in dark corners. But
not this time. This time he'd actually be able to share
the TRUTH! The magic! The joy! The wonder!

**20 MINUTES AFTER** the reported gunfire,
two patrolmen approached with gats drawn.

They'd been parked on MacDougal eating bagged
suppers when their windshield had been jubilantly
rapped. While their snitch had enabled myriad collars
— suicides endowed zero grist. Mountains of paper...
glory bereft...Algernon's customary sawbuck reward
had been surrendered amidst abject despair.

"Fuck...really wanna face dis t'night?"

"Nope."

"Me neitha. But...shit...if dat rummy sells
it t'Flanagan too, an' HE finds out we had it
foist...den it's MY ass in a waxpapah sling!
Guy's brotha-in-law brokahed my mortgage!"

"But Algy prolly ain't gonna squawk. Why
hep anudda fella youse hawkin' used dope?
Den youse can't fuckin' sell it...correct?"

Eyeballs hairy studied each other.

"Cause mushbrain jigs don't know bettah..."

Burgers were finished in silence.

**ENTERING HIS NEST** beneath the Hangman's
Elm, Michael Rat was dismayed to find his wife de-
vouring a litter freshbirthed — a task she approached
with such rapturous zeal his homecoming was scarcely
noted. Dragging pulp through a narrow porthole,
he paused with the wad teethclenched.

**SPOTTING THE MOONLIT CORPSE**, the smaller
cop jostled the larger. "Whoa, Frank! Big gun aloit!"
   Torches aimed atop knees splayed illumed
a Colt beneath a limp claw.
   "Got dat right! Cannon! Dem t'ings went out with da
RoughRidahs! Lissen, Joe — jus' do me a solid?
Handle dis? Can't see dis right afta I ate..."
   "Jesus Christ, man — me fuckin' too!"
   "Think mebbe he's jus' sleepin' one off? I mean...
smells liked he bathed in Rheingold."
   "Yeah an' mebbe I'm fuckin' Roland La Starza!
Look at dat blood...dis fella's WAY past defunct!"
   "Alright den, so we do it togetha. Copacetic?"

**MICHAEL RAT WANTED** to weep.
   Viscera dangled from Minerva's mouthcorners.
   Her whiskers were slickened with bile.
   Dropping his treasure, earth ruining its taste, he
mournfully sighed then slowly crept forwards to gnaw.

**BENT AS IF HINGED,** the corpse's head laid atop
urinesoaked thighs; blood pouring from each orifice.
   Red tears clotted smashed lenses.
   A pool welled betwixt Florsheims.
   Fecal scents conquered supreme —
the atmosphere reeking of garbage.

Lowering a hand to a hunched shoulder, the smaller cop gently shook — lilting with the same mindful whisper he employed to tuck his own spawn.

"Psst buddy...y'okay? Too many drinkypoos?"
Witness-scanning, the larger cop clucked.
"Christ, dis guy's definitely dead."
"No shit, Einstein — dat's what I said!"
"Really t'ink he did it hisself?"
"Ain't dat da gun right fuckin' dere?
Youse glim dat green shit on his fingah?"
"Dunno...nevah seen triggas leave no mark like dat."
"Course it's from a trigga! Said so y'self — dat rod's way old! Or maybe youse'd like even MORE typin'?"
"S'already a lotta typin' eitha way."
"What is? I don't see nothin'...do youse?"
"Go for a Pepsi?"

**A HORSEFLY EMERGING** from the corpse's left nostril trailed the pair back to their cruiser.

# TIGER MOODY IS STUPID, UGLY, BOORISH & SMELLY. HE LIVES AND WORKS IN LOWER MANHATTAN.

www.ingramcontent.com/pod-product-compliance
Lightning Source LLC
Chambersburg PA
CBHW032015170626
46807CB00006B/2820